"Don't Walk Away From Me."

Shocked at his audacity, Madeline could only stare and try not to quail at the storm in her new boss's eyes.

"The people of this town will suffer if you do anything stupid like resigning. You think I care about a few run-down hotels? I'll close them like *that!*" He snapped his fingers.

Behind him the elevator doors closed and silence descended. Madeline knew she had to clear her head, take stock, think. But his proximity in the confined space set her heart thundering in excitement.

"What do you want?" she whispered.

"What do I want?" His voice softened considerably. The light in his eyes changed to something even more dangerous. More dangerous because she'd seen it before....

Dear Reader,

A special friend of mine is moving from the house she has lived in for fifty-four years, since the day she married. Her babies spent their first days here and now her grandchildren play with their parents' toys. Anniversaries, milestone birthdays; comings and goings and teens necking in the garage; wrenching times at the passing of those before their time: All those memories hoarded away are now elbowed awake to be sorted into piles. But stay or go, they'll live on in someone's mind. This won't be their last hurrah.

It's a brave decision to move a life. Her daughters shed a tear or two but totally support her decision to move into something smaller, warmer, cleaner, newer, because they know that Daph will take home with her. She *is* home.

My heroine didn't have a happy childhood home, but she couldn't settle anywhere until she realized we all need the comfort of memories and the prospect of making new ones. Memories that will last for the next fifty years and be rudely awakened one day just for the pleasure of passing them on and keeping them alive.

Happy memories!

Jan Colley

JAN COLLEY

BILLIONAIRE'S FAVORITE FANTASY

Published by Silhouette Books

America's Publisher of Contemporary Romance

 SILHOUETTE BOOKS

ISBN-13: 978-0-373-76882-0
ISBN-10:   0-373-76882-6

BILLIONAIRE'S FAVORITE FANTASY

Visit Silhouette Books at www.eHarlequin.com

Printed in U.S.A.

Books by Jan Colley

Silhouette Desire

Trophy Wives #1698
Melting the Icy Tycoon #1770
Expecting a Fortune #1795
Satin & a Scandalous Affair #1861
Billionaire's Favorite Fantasy #1882

JAN COLLEY

lives in Christchurch, New Zealand, with Les and a couple of cats. She has traveled extensively, is jack of all trades and master of none and still doesn't know what she wants to be when she grows up—as long as it's a writer. She loves rugby, family and friends, writing, sunshine, talking about writing, and cats, although not necessarily in that order. E-mail her at vagabond232@yahoo.com or check out her Web site at www.jancolley.com.

To Les

One

"It is with great pleasure that I introduce Madeline Holland, our new chief operating officer, based in Sydney."

As the smattering of polite applause died away, the acting chair peered over his specs down the table at her. "Please tell us a little about yourself, my dear. I know you spent many years with Global Hospitality…"

Madeline returned his smile, smoothed the skirt of her smart burgundy skirt and started to rise.

Suddenly the door flew open and banged against its stop with a crack. All eyes swiveled to assess the intrusion. Beside her, Madeline felt her best friend, Kay, tense and prepare to rise. Kay was regional manager of the three Premier Hotels here in Queenstown, New Zealand, so security came under her domain.

A tall, lean, impeccably dressed man stood framed by the doorway, holding a stack of glossy files. Half standing, half crouching, Madeline glanced at his face and her throat snapped shut. Dear God, it was him! Her fantasy lover of the night before.

The punch of adrenaline rocked her all the way to her heels. Her smile froze as she stared at his longish dark-blond hair, the model stubble along his jaw, his aquiline nose and sharply cut upper lip. She closed her eyes, remembering mesmerizing sea-green eyes, hazed over with passion but now thankfully hidden by sunglasses.

No, no, no…

Her breath came back in a strangled gasp and she eased herself back down in her seat, praying the floor would open up and swallow her. Had he known who she was? As she'd writhed in his strong arms during the night, had he, even then, been thinking about crashing this closed meeting today?

She shrank in her seat.

The man gave a cursory all-inclusive glance around the boardroom table and moved forward into the room. "Good afternoon, ladies and gentlemen. My name is Lewis Goode." He commenced handing out files while Madeline kept her eyes resolutely lowered. Would he acknowledge her? Would he smile, smug in the knowledge that he'd seen her sans clothing, inhibitions, coherence? Her heart pounded against her rib cage.

His hands now empty, he strode to the front and offered his hand to the acting chair, who smiled broadly, and took a seat at the side of the table.

Lewis Goode took off his sunglasses, slipping them into his inside pocket, raised his head and surveyed the table. "Some of you here will know me."

He gave a brief smile at the six places on both sides closest to him, made up mostly of the directors of the board. Then he lifted his head to take in the rest of the Executive Committee.

Madeline hunched even lower, her fingers gripping the table edge lest she lose her nerve and bolt. She shouldn't even be here since she was not a member of the Executive Committee. Neither was Kay, but as she'd organized the annual conference here in Queenstown, she had asked for permission to attend and bring Madeline along to be introduced as the newest member of the team.

"For those who don't know me," the man said, "I am now the majority shareholder and new chief executive of Premier Hotel Group."

A collective gasp rose up from Madeline's half of the table, but most of the directors up front did not look surprised. Madeline, however, fought against covering her mouth lest she groan out loud.

She had slept with her new boss.

"Yesterday morning," Lewis continued, "the Australian Securities and Investments Commission approved the corporate takeover I initiated a year ago. For those of you on the board who supported me, I thank you. For those who didn't—" he paused ominously as the assembled guests cast surreptitious glances toward the top of the table "—there is nothing I admire more than loyalty—to me. If you cannot commit to that, then you only have to make your position known and I will see that you get a fair termination package."

All eyes scrutinized the implacable faces of the directors of the board.

"As with any corporate takeover, we are embarking on a settling-in period," Lewis Goode continued. "There will be reviews, and all executives will be required to reapply for their jobs."

Her friend Kay turned to her, a look of dismay and apology on her face. Kay didn't realize it but she had more to apologize for than persuading Madeline to give up a perfectly good job to apply for the Premier Hotels position. She had also unwittingly provided the magical setting for Madeline's indiscretion last night.

But at the time, it had felt so uncannily right…

"Except," Lewis went on, "for the man I've replaced, Jacques de Vries, whose contract is terminated immediately." Again a gasp went around most of the table. Jacques de Vries was iconic, the founder of this massive global hotel company. "And—" Lewis paused and looked straight at Madeline, sending her nerves jangling in panic "—Madeline Holland, who will take up her position as COO, Australia and New Zealand division, as planned."

Madeline's breath huffed out and she tore her eyes from his face. Kay's somber expression lightened considerably, her relief evident that she hadn't persuaded Madeline to return to the Southern Hemisphere after twelve years away, only to be made redundant.

Madeline envied her friend her ignorance. How, she wondered, agonizingly close to tears, could she ever live this down?

Her gut jumped again as she realized Lewis Goode's eyes still bored into her face. Get me out of here, she prayed.

Lewis smiled thinly, as if he could clearly see the path of her thoughts. "Your reputation in operations and administration precedes you, Ms. Holland. Your first job will be to relocate the head office of Premier from Singapore to Sydney. I look forward to working closely with you on that."

Kay nudged her, smiling, but Madeline was still reeling from the force of his gaze and his smile; the inflection he placed on the word *closely*—and from the fact that he had just given himself away. *Your reputation precedes you...* So he had known exactly who she was last night.

Somehow she pasted a semblance of a smile onto her mouth and held it there, but confusion and a slow-burning anger nipped at the heels of her panic.

Finally Lewis took his eyes off her hot face. "I look forward to getting to know all of you over the next few days while we enjoy the annual Premier conference in this beautiful part of New Zealand's South Island. But now, I would like to talk to the board of directors, so if everyone else would kindly excuse us."

A flurry of chairs scraping and excited whispers ensued while everyone not at the head of the table rose and collected papers and briefcases. Madeline kept her head down and forced herself not to push as she made for the door. Thankfully, once outside, Kay was diverted by several colleagues, giving Madeline a chance to regroup and compose herself.

The delegates huddled around Kay. "Did you know about this?"

Kay shook her head. "I've heard rumors but I don't think anyone expected it so soon."

Madeline leaned against the wall, the conversation largely washing over her. Everyone wanted to know how this could have happened or, more important, how the powerful Jacques de Vries could have allowed it to happen.

Madeline couldn't care less about the former CEO. She wanted to know what the new CEO had been thinking of when he'd whisked her to bed last night. Unbidden, her mind bombarded her with myriad images of well-honed muscle and sinew over tanned skin, the feel of him wedged deep inside her body, his lips pulled back in a grimace of ecstasy.

She pressed against the wall, her nipples tingling with the memory. Twenty-eight years old and she hugged a wall, feeling ashamed and insignificant. She was transported back twelve years to another episode of her own making, the one that instigated her decision to leave her mother, friends and home town. Madeline had worked tirelessly to erase the insecure, inhibited girl she'd been. And she thought she'd been successful.

Oh, why had she let Lewis Goode seduce her last night?

Kay broke away from the group and turned to her. "I could use a drink," she muttered. "My office or the bar?"

Madeline pushed away from the wall. "Office." Anywhere, she thought, away from people.

"I'm sorry, hon. I didn't see this coming." Kay stopped at her secretary's desk and looked at Madeline. "Is chardonnay okay?"

Madeline nodded and Kay requested a bottle and two glasses be brought up from the bar.

They continued on into Kay's office.

"I should have warned you this was a possibility."

Madeline shrugged. How could she be anything but grateful to her old school friend? While she'd been relentlessly climbing the corporate ladder, it was Kay who'd kept an eye on her mother, who notified her of the old woman's slide into Alzheimer's disease, who'd persuaded Madeline to apply for a job closer to home. She'd even organized her mother's move into the retirement village.

Kay plopped down behind her desk, gesturing for Madeline to sit. "I honestly thought—we all did—that Jacques was way too strong to let something like this happen. He started this company, you know." Kay raised her cell phone and began to text expertly. "Obviously the board of directors thought differently."

Madeline had never met the former CEO, but his name was legend in the hotel industry. Premier Hotel Group was largely Australasian but there were a smattering of hotels in the United States, where her old company, Global Hospitality, was based.

Kay's face brightened. "You must be relieved not to have to reapply. I wonder if that applies to regional managers."

"Your guess is as good as mine," Madeline murmured distractedly. "Tell me about Lewis Goode." After all, she only knew the little stuff, like the naked desire in his eyes as he'd slowly undressed her, the heat of his skin when she touched him. His clever hands and mouth... "I've heard his name, I think—" Not last night, she hadn't... "—but I didn't realize he had anything to do with the hotel industry."

"He doesn't, to my knowledge." Kay waved her fingers vaguely at the coffee table behind Madeline, where she kept her stash of business magazines. Madeline riffled through a couple.

Her heartbeat kicked up when Lewis Goode's

handsome, somber face stared up at her from the second magazine. She obviously read the wrong business publications. The face was unforgettable.

"He owns a lot of companies, notably Pacific Star Airlines," her friend went on. "Bought it for a song about five years ago, and now it's the second biggest airline in the Pacific."

Madeline stopped poring over the photo and flicked to the article, justifying her ignorance by acknowledging the geographical distance. After all, she'd been based in the States and came home rarely. And she'd only applied for the Premier job less than a month ago.

How did he know who she was? And why didn't he disclose his identity? Never mind that in the surreal ambiance of the Alpine Fantasy Retreat, the scene of last night's unexpected rendezvous, they'd playfully decided not to divulge any personal details to each other, including their names. What was he hoping to gain, apart from a cheap thrill? Madeline wasn't in a position to assist with the corporate takeover.

She was, however, in an unenviable situation. "Hopefully he'll play with his planes and leave the hotel business to those who know it."

"From what I've heard, he's sharp—a hands-on boss," Kay commented.

Oh, if only you knew, Madeline thought.

"It's me who should be worried," Kay said grimly. "Just between us—and since you're my new boss,

I'm trusting you, here—we're really struggling. Pray for a fantastic ski season."

Madeline stopped wallowing in self-pity long enough to take in her friend's words. Both women had started at the bottom and, over the years, worked their way up through the ranks, studying in their free time to get ahead. Madeline advanced her career with a different hotel chain, travelling, taking the postings no one else wanted, to reach a level of success she could only have dreamed about. Kay made regional manager last year after a decade in the trade, barring a year off when her twins were born.

"Even if things aren't great," Madeline reasoned, "he wouldn't be a very savvy CEO if he pulled Premier from the number-one tourist destination in New Zealand."

Queenstown's reputation as an adventure playground and ski resort gave it the happy dilemma that it didn't have an off season. There were literally hundreds of accommodation options to choose from in the tiny town. Premier, with its Waterfront, Lakeside and Mountainview Hotels, held prime positions in the town. In fact, when she and Kay started in the business, the three Premier Hotels were the single largest employer in town.

The door opened and Kay's secretary entered, carrying a tray with a bottle and two glasses. "There is a Mr. Lewis Goode outside to see you. He doesn't have an appointment."

Madeline's head rose so sharply, she heard her neck click. Here? She hurriedly rose, looking for a means of escape.

Kay exhaled noisily, raising her brows at Madeline. "Okay. Another glass, Felicity."

Please, please, let the earth swallow me now.

Lewis walked straight to Kay's desk, his hand outstretched and a semi-smile on his lips. Madeline hovered to the side, pressing her damp palms down her hips.

"I thought we should meet before the conference starts," Lewis said to Kay. "I understand you are the event organiser this year."

"Yes." Kay sounded almost relaxed. "Just one of my many talents. Have you officially met Madeline Holland?"

Lewis turned to Madeline and her heart leapt with velocity into her throat. His green eyes were cool and assessing, as opposed to hot and wanting. His mouth curved on one side in what she perceived to be a wolfish amusement.

"Not officially, no." He held out his hand. "Madeline."

She took his hand briefly, aware that hers probably felt like a damp squib. His was warm, dry and came with a businesslike squeeze, but when he released her, she felt the pressure remain as if he hadn't let go.

"You were at Global Hospitality for ten years, yes?"

Madeline nodded, afraid that to speak would be to squeak.

"What brought you to Premier?" he asked.

"I—" Madeline tried to swallow the lump of nerves lodged in her throat "—wanted to be closer to home."

He arched a brow. "Home?"

"My mother is in a retirement village here."

"Madeline and I grew up together," Kay put in helpfully. "In fact, we both started right here in the Premier Waterfront as part-time housemaids when we were sixteen."

Both his pale brows rose as he still looked down on Madeline's face. "I didn't know that."

The door behind them opened, and Kay's secretary entered, carrying another wineglass.

"You'll join us, I hope." Kay said. "We're having a welcome-home drink for Madeline."

For a few agonizingly hopeful seconds, Madeline thought he would decline. But then he turned to Kay, a smile warming his face. "If you're sure I'm not intruding."

"Not at all." She picked up the bottle and began to pour while Madeline focused on the amber liquid slipping into the bowl of the glass. Anything not to dwell on the widening smile on his face. She wondered if wolves, like cats, liked to play with their prey before delivering the killing blow.

"And are you enjoying your visit home so far, Madeline?" Lewis asked politely. To her it seemed his voice was full of intent, stroking over the syllables of her name, rendering it exotic, seductive, while she'd always considered it stuffy and old-fashioned.

But then his words sunk into her brain and she knew what he meant. *Did you enjoy last night, Madeline?*

Lewis Goode was going to milk this for all he was worth. She inhaled carefully and inclined her head on a neck that felt like a pole of steel.

Kay passed a glass of wine to each of them, her eyes lingering on Madeline's with a loaded look confirming her stuffed-dummy impression. She wrapped her fingers around her glass tightly, trying to erase the feel of his hand on hers.

Kay coughed. "Will you be staying for the conference, Mr. Goode?"

Smiling, Lewis turned away from Madeline. "It's Lewis. And yes, for a few days."

"Queenstown is the adrenaline capital of the world," Kay prattled on heroically. "I've organized some pretty wild activities, my way of getting some revenge on all you executives."

Lewis smiled. "We should enjoy that, shouldn't we, Madeline?"

Her head rose. "I'm on holiday at the moment." Her eyes slid away from the relentless green gaze and she sipped her wine. "I start on the first of next month."

Lewis's smile was polite, but she heard the steel in his voice. "Not too busy for the annual conference, I hope."

She bit down on a retort, but her heart sank. While Kay and her new boss chatted, she stood silently, ruminating on irony. All her hopes of reaching the pinnacle of success, a triumphant homecoming, dashed. If this got out—and it would get out—how could she face the people of Queenstown, her mother or her new staff in Sydney?

Lewis sipped his wine and enjoyed Madeline's discomfort, listening with one ear to Kay's prattling.

Madeline Holland was a world-class actress, he'd give her that. Even in the throes of indescribable passion, she'd given no indication she knew who he was. Jacques had chosen his seductress well.

But that was Jacques de Vries to a T. Always one step ahead of everyone else—until this morning.

Lewis took another satisfying draught of wine. Today was the culmination of two years of planning and hard work. He'd gotten most of the directors onboard months ago, but had been forced to cool his impatient heels while the government's business watchdog completed its investigation and agreed that the deal was sound and of full disclosure.

Jacques's apoplectic face swam before his eyes, and he almost smiled. Lewis wasn't a cruel man, but in this case, vengeance was sweet. Jacques had believed himself so strong, so untouchable that no one could harm him. He'd learned today that no one was bulletproof, especially those who surrounded themselves with toadies and people accustomed to jumping on the backs of the strong in order to feather their nests.

"You mistook their loathing for fear and respect, Jacques," he'd told the old man earlier, before ordering him out of his presidential suite and the hotel. "The directors were easy to sway."

He glanced at the uncomfortable woman standing two feet away, unwilling to meet his eyes. When he'd left her this morning, he'd forced her from his mind because there was work to be done. Now he indulged in a moment of reflection.

Her lashes and brows were dark, her hair a mane of silky gold, although it was pulled back into a neat knot now. An unusual beauty spot accentuated her high cheekbones and perfect honeyed skin. Lewis had pressed his lips to it while she slept when he'd left her this morning. He inhaled, all his senses remembering and warming to her elegant fragrance. Her thick brows knit together in perplexity, and she kept her cobalt-blue eyes directed at her feet.

Yes, Madeline Holland was memorable. He'd intended to keep her on after reading her file because of her reputation in the industry and the fact that she would have no loyalty to the old regime and would be easy to mould. Sleeping with her was a most unexpected and welcome bonus.

Lewis had known chemistry before, but Madeline's pull on his senses was easily the most intense of his life. He'd gone to the Alpine Fantasy Retreat to keep a low profile until today's meeting. When the Kiwi beauty sneaked into his private space, he'd played along with Jacques's silly ploy to send in his spy. He took his fill of her charms, again and again, and now had staked his claim for the company she worked for.

Satisfied beyond measure, Lewis widened his smile to include her. She'd earned her bonus and then some, although her panicked expression when he walked into the boardroom earlier had elicited a pang of sympathy from him. How was he supposed to know she'd be at the meeting? She wasn't listed on the Executive Committee.

Lewis realized Kay was waiting for him to answer a question and took his eyes off Madeline. "Sorry?"

Kay asked if he intended to utilize the speech time Jacques de Vries had been allocated at the Gala Opening the following night.

"Of course," he affirmed, "though I doubt I will be quite so long-winded." He checked his watch and set his half-empty glass down on the desk. Dusk bathed the lake outside Kay's office window in an eerie purple bruise. He knew the roads iced up early and it was a forty-minute drive to the Retreat. "Kay, I'd like to move into the top floor tomorrow. I hear the presidential suite is vacant." He ignored Madeline's sharp inhalation, but it confirmed his suspicions that she was probably accommodated in the hotel. "And I'd like you to find some time in your busy schedule over the next few days to discuss your operation here."

Lewis thanked her for the drink and said goodbye, saying he'd see them at the Gala Ball to open the conference tomorrow night.

Madeline's mumbled comment that she wasn't sure if she was going elicited a sound of dismay from Kay, but Lewis only nodded at both of them.

"I'll see you both there," he said firmly.

Two

The next night Madeline laid her knife and fork down and gazed around the ballroom of the Premier Waterfront Hotel. Kay's inspired midwinter Christmas theme dazzled, complete with a massive, sumptuously decorated tree. Large circular tables accommodated the five hundred delegates in front of a mezzanine stage. It was a visual masterpiece with stars overhead, a digitally generated cornucopia of ever-changing Christmas themes dancing around the walls, and columns of silver mesh lights hanging from the eight-meter ceiling.

Each of the ten-place, linen-clothed tables had a small Christmas tree as the centerpiece and gaily wrapped gifts at every place-setting. Kay had outdone herself, Madeline thought admiringly, watching her friend on the stage welcoming the guests as the formal part of the evening commenced. The banquet impressed everyone at her table, and the wines were top of the range.

Madeline looked around at the beautiful dresses and tuxedos of the high-powered executives from all over the world and knew she could never have organized such a glittering event. "She's wasted in hotels," she murmured to John, Kay's proud husband, seated beside her. "Event management is her forte."

She glanced over to the head table where Lewis Goode sat with the board of directors, waiting for Kay to introduce him. The rumors about the new CEO's plans for the town's hotels had already begun. Would he give her friend a fair hearing or had he made up his mind already about the reportedly unprofitable Queenstown hotels? She set her mouth grimly. He would have her to answer to if he tried to get rid of Kay.

The subject of her thoughts strode up onto the stage and shook Kay's hand warmly.

"Most events of this size," he began, "take an Olympic-size team of event coordinators to do what Kay has achieved with her small band of hotel staff. It is testament to the regard in which she is held in this community that she has been able to put everything together with such vision and style."

Beaming, Kay left the stage and took her place next to her husband and Madeline. For the first time, Lewis Goode faced most of the executives of his multinational corporation.

Madeline watched him captivate the crowd so intently for the next twenty minutes, you might have heard a pin drop in the huge ballroom. Despite her conflicted feelings, she couldn't help admiring his supremely confident bearing and impressive business knowledge. No one hearing him could doubt that he was a man with high expectations, who knew exactly where he was going. He urged everyone to work together with him to bring Premier once again to the forefront of the world-wide hotel industry.

"For too long," he said, "this company has been hamstrung by a few at the top living it up to the detriment of everyone. In the past few years, expansion has stalled, maintenance neglected, recruitment and training ignored. Join me in welcoming the winds of change." Judging by the applause this missive received, clearly most of the international delegates agreed with his assessment. Madeline wondered whether the local population would be so enthused with all this talk of change.

He left the stage to a rousing ovation, words like *charisma* and *magnetism* whispered enthusiastically around the tables.

"Wow!" Kay turned to her, rolling her eyes. "I'd follow him into battle any day."

Reluctantly Madeline agreed. How could she tell her friend she'd been burned with the same charisma and magnetism, but in a much more personal venue? Her shameful secret weighed like an anchor on her chest and she longed to share, but Kay had enough on her plate with the conference plus the threat of Lewis inspecting the hotels under her jurisdiction in the next day or two.

"Speaking of wow," Kay continued, pointing to Madeline's cocktail dress. "Would your mother approve of that dress, Madeline the Good?" They laughed at the high school nickname that had dogged her for years.

Madeline's mother owned the dubious distinction of being the town kook, dubbed the "Bible Lady" for her habit of standing on street corners haranguing people about the evils of liquor and sex. Madeline grew up being either ridiculed or pitied by her peers. Friends were discouraged, her school uniform draped her like a sack, and her mother cut her hair. As for makeup, her mother called that the devil's pride. The older she got, the more excruciating the teasing, but her mother seemed oblivious.

Madeline smoothed down the charcoal-satin cocktail dress, tugging at the bubble hem that stopped just above her knees. "You chose it," she grumbled, reminding Kay of their shopping trip last month when she'd come to Sydney to offer moral support for Madeline's interview.

"Relax. You look great," her friend said as Madeline fidgeted with the bodice that enhanced her modest cleavage. There was no sense regretting the purchase. Her belongings were en route from her last posting to the Darling Harbour Premier Hotel in Sydney, her bolthole until she found an apartment. She had nothing else suitable for a function like this.

Kay turned to speak to someone at the neighboring table. A strange prickle of unease skittered up Madeline's spine, as though someone was watching her. Involuntarily, her eyes drifted over to where Lewis sat with high-ranking members of the board of directors. His eyes raked her even as he bent his head toward one of his cronies and appeared to be listening intently.

Madeline looked away hurriedly and wondered how she could have made such a huge blunder. She *was* a good girl, who'd never escaped the inhibitions imprinted on her by her straitlaced mother. Her love life was a joke. Over the years, she'd worked insane hours to study for the qualifications she needed to win her impressive cache of promotions. Her professionalism kept temptation at bay in the office, and since work was her life, there were few other opportunities. Sexual encounters were rare, on vacation, away from any semblance of the familiar and anyone she may know. Sweet, short, and most of all secret.

Okay, technically she had been on holiday at the Alpine Fantasy Retreat, but to sleep with a stranger after knowing him only a few hours, with her home town just a few miles away, was stupid in the extreme.

Madeline was nothing like the woman Lewis Goode thought she was.

A band struck up on the stage, the lights dimmed, and the atmosphere changed from business to pleasure. Beside her, Kay and John conversed quietly. Madeline idly tapped the lip of her champagne flute against her mouth, looking around at her new colleagues, none of whom she knew. Perhaps she might slip away soon. She'd had little enough sleep at the retreat two nights ago, and her dreams last night were peppered with ominous images.

"Bored, Ms. Holland?"

Lewis Goode eased his long frame into the empty chair beside her, his presence instigating a flurry of nerves. She focused on steadying her hand as she set her glass down. "Not at all," she said with a sideways glance at Kay, who was still deep in conversation with her husband. "I was about to leave, actually."

Lewis frowned and glanced at his watch. "Before dessert and not even ten o'clock. Do we want to give the impression that the new COO is a lightweight?"

Her shoulders lifted—until she remembered the cleavage perpetuated by this dress. "I didn't intend staying long." Forcing her eyes up above his throat, she met his gaze.

His eyes crinkled at the corners. "It would be a shame to take that dress home without at least one twirl around the dance floor." He stood up and put his hand out.

Madeline closed her eyes briefly, wishing she was anywhere else in the world. His presence alone was enough to remind her of her lack of judgment. Spending one second in his arms with everyone watching would be torture.

But Lewis stood smiling easily, somehow knowing she wasn't the type to make a scene.

With a petulant sigh for his ears only, she stood and slid her arm through his, ignoring his hand. They walked stiffly to the dance floor.

As he turned her toward him and slid a hand around her waist, she successfully absorbed the wild palpitations in her chest at his touch, enough, she hoped, not to raise any eyebrows.

"Why are you doing this?" she asked quietly, focusing over his shoulder.

Lewis tilted his head toward her and she had to physically check herself from ducking back as a delicious wave of sexy male scent, familiar but forbidden, washed over her.

"Dancing with my COO?" he asked lightly. "We're the newbies here. Best we stick together."

Madeline listened carefully for some sardonic inflection or twist to his words but couldn't identify it.

"You have quite a reputation in this small town," he continued, his lips only centimeters from her ear.

Her heart took a dive. So he'd heard of her teenage

disgrace, the reason she'd left. Perhaps that was why he'd made a play for her at the retreat: a woman of loose morals and one he held a position of power over. Or possibly, he'd just heard about her mother's eccentricities.

"Everywhere I turn," Lewis said in a low voice, "people are saying 'little Miss Holland, hasn't she done well?'"

Madeline knew that most of them would have tacked "considering" onto the end of that, but a smile still ghosted over her lips. She'd kept away for years, wondering if she'd ever be accepted here. Landing the job based in Sydney, Australia, seemed like the best option. She could keep her distance, but still be close enough to rush home if her mother's health deteriorated.

Lewis leaned back slightly so he could look down into her face. "You're a little uptight tonight. Let's indulge in some party talk. Seen any good movies lately?"

Not fair! His sly reference to their first meeting at the Alpine Fantasy Retreat's private movie theatre, churned up a ripe pique that had her pressing her lips together.

Her vain hope that he may be as embarrassed as she about their sordid little fling was dashed. Lewis Goode did not believe in gallantry, obviously. Just like a man, she thought savagely. He clearly did not share her view that acting on something as primal as pure lust diminished both of them, not just her.

"Did you know who I was when you seduced me at the retreat?" she clipped out as he twirled her around.

Lewis's eyes warmed. "I seduced you? Hmm. I rather thought it was a mutual decision."

"Did you know?" she demanded in a fierce whisper.

He inclined his head. "I'd seen the executives files. You made a charming spy."

"What do you mean, spy?"

A steely glint flashed in his eye. "Come, Ms. Holland. Jacques put you there at the lodge to keep an eye on me."

Madeline somehow managed to keep moving, albeit stiffly. There was no way she wanted their colleagues to suspect there was anything more than a working relationship going on. But the bitter realization that he thought she was nothing more than Jacques de Vries's prostitute, lashed hard. "For your information, Mr. Goode, I never even met Jacques de Vries. The retreat was a welcome-home present from Kay. Ask her, if you don't believe me." Madeline arched slightly away from him, her stilted steps a lame excuse for dancing. How abhorrent that he thought she would sleep with him because her boss asked her to. She kept her eyes down, trying to swallow righteous anger and calm her breathing.

Lewis's grip on her fingers tightened and then his thigh nudged hers, blanking her mind with a speedy flush of sexual energy that seemed to flow from her to him and back again. Not now, she thought despairingly, when she needed her wits about her like never before.

He pulled her closer. "Dance," he muttered.

Somehow, she forced her feet to move, her spine to loosen, but she couldn't do much about the burn of hot blood to her cheeks.

Lewis inhaled deeply, his chest rising. "You must appreciate the coincidence," he said quietly, close to her ear. "No one knew I was in town. I planned to keep a low profile until the meeting, and there you were."

"My key…" she whispered heatedly, but what was the point? He knew she'd left her key on the seat in the theatre and that is what led to their portentous meeting.

While she strove for composure, he ducked his head and looked into her eyes for several moments. Then he straightened, sighing. "All right, in the interests of forging an amicable working relationship with my right-hand man, as it were, I'll give you the benefit of the doubt." He shrugged nonchalantly. "Consider it forgotten."

"Forgotten?" If only! "Forgotten that you had me at a disadvantage by knowing my identity while not revealing yours?"

His arm tightened around her waist again, bringing his body so close, she felt the muscles shift and ripple in his upper thighs.

"No names, remember?" He smiled tightly. "I believe that was your idea."

Madeline blinked. He was right. In a mind splintered by reckless sexual attraction, she'd suggested they play along with the magical spell the place cast and not divulge identities or personal details. The only direct question she'd asked was if he lived in Queenstown. He was obviously Australian and he told her he was here on business.

That was all she'd wanted to know. What he did, who his loved ones were, what consequences there might be of a coupling based on lust only, did not interest her. She knew within minutes of meeting him that they would finish the day in her big four-poster bed. They'd walked, talked, eaten dinner and drunk wine. It was five hours before he kissed her the first time. Shortly after that, she drowned in passion.

It sounded tawdry, but it hadn't been that way, not one minute of it. Not at the time. "Are you—are you going to tell?"

He raised his brows. "Kiss and tell, you mean?" His eyes drifted to her mouth and lingered there. "You must admit, it gives me some leverage, and I could use an ally."

Madeline blanched and tried to tug her hand away, but Lewis tightened his grip, indicating the other dancers with his chin.

"If idle gossip distresses you, I suggest you stop making a scene and make this dance look slightly more as if we are newly acquainted business colleagues."

Madeline stilled, hating the fact that he spoke sense. Breathe, she ordered herself. Move.

"That's better," he murmured, still not looking at her.

She willed her body to relax, and it obeyed and flowed in the direction he took them. Lewis was a good dancer, but she already knew that from the other night. They'd danced to a different tune then, a slow-moving soul number that brought sultriness into a cabin deep in snow-covered mountains. The memory of it, coupled with the heat of his hand around her waist, his thigh nudging hers, made her tingle and burn.

How was she ever to work with this man when his every look and touch reminded her of what they'd done? Overwhelmed by his magnetism, she hated herself for wanting him as she did.

"This isn't going to work," she muttered, not caring whether he heard or not.

Lewis smiled grimly. "You're better than that, Madeline. You didn't get to where you are by being lily-livered."

Maybe not, but she'd never felt an attraction of this magnitude before.

"Besides," he went on, lowering his head so his mouth brushed her ear, sending a shiver through her. "I think I have self-control enough to keep my hands to myself in the office. And if I can't, then we'll just have to alter your job description."

Bastard!

She injected some steel into her spine, knowing if she didn't stand up for herself now, she didn't have a hope of having a career in his company. And she wanted that, more than anything—didn't she? "My position is confirmed, Mr. Goode. You said so yourself."

"As I recall, you can be quite flexible when it comes to your—position."

Something in her died. There was no respect here. There never would be. Madeline stepped back, dragging her hand from his. Who cared what their colleagues thought? His colleagues, she amended silently. "This really isn't going to work. You will have my resignation in the morning."

She turned abruptly and strode away from him as fast as she could in three-inch heels, pausing only long enough to snatch her purse off her table and give a terse nod at a surprised-looking Kay.

She stalked from the ballroom, but seeing Kay brought the realization home of what she was giving up. What had she done? Her dream job, the prize for which she'd worked so hard. How could she be so stupid, so spineless, to let him goad her into resigning?

It surprised her that he could be so callous. They'd talked, too, at that Alpine retreat, it wasn't just sex. Only in the most general terms: what they wanted, what was stopping them, likes and dislikes. How could he listen to her hopes and dreams and make love to her with such absorbing intensity, and now treat her like a plaything?

Her heels clicked sharply on the marble floor of the hotel foyer as she made for the bank of elevators. She clutched her evening purse in a death grip, imagining her fingers around his neck, squeezing hard. But really, her anger and humiliation were directed at herself. What man would turn down a willing partner in a no-strings fling? And even now, blinded by dismay and disappointment, she still wanted him, wanted him to want her.

The elevator doors swished open and she stepped inside, desperate to be alone. But suddenly, Lewis was there, his broad shoulders taking up all the space, squeezing through the closing doors and looming purposefully over her. Making her dizzy with shock and excitement.

"Oh, no, you don't," he muttered. "You don't walk away from me. And don't even *think* about resigning. I won't have it."

Shocked at his audacity, she could only stare and try not to quail at the storm in his eyes.

"The people of this town will suffer—your friend Kay will suffer—if you do anything stupid like resigning."

Her mouth dropped open. "Wh-what? How?"

His tone was grim. "You think I care about a few run-down hotels at the bottom of the world? I will close these three hotels like that!" He snapped his fingers under her nose.

Behind him the elevator doors closed and silence descended, except for the sound of her heart pounding. Since neither had pressed the buttons, this car was going nowhere. Just like her career.

"You wouldn't." She hardly recognized her own voice, thin and thready.

"That's where you're wrong," he grated. "Premier's name in this town is a standing joke. We'd be better off cutting our losses."

Madeline knew she had to clear her head, take stock, think! Or else her friend would really have something to worry about. But his proximity in the confined space set her heart thundering in excitement.

"What do you want?" she whispered.

"What do I want?" His voice softened considerably by the end of the short sentence. The light in his eyes changed to something even more dangerous than his threats to close the hotels. More dangerous because she'd seen it before, just before he kissed her for the first time.

As if to underscore the point, his hand lifted to brush her cheek, telling her what she'd just finished admitting to herself.

"You've already had that," she whispered hoarsely, praying she'd be able to resist.

"Did you really think that one night was ever going to be enough?" The tip of his tongue flicked out to lick his bottom lip while he stared at her mouth hungrily.

"You despised me when you thought I was Jacques's prostitute," she told him, holding on to her control, the last vestige of anger by a thread. "Now you want me to be your exclusive prostitute?"

"Strange, isn't it?" He stepped forward, breaching

her last defense. "I keep thinking walk away, but then I see you, get close enough to touch and smell…"

Her heart pitched to the ceiling, then settled back down as an ominous fatalism told her she wouldn't—couldn't—resist. Not when he was this close, taking her air, her power of thought and reason. It was as if she was his to command.

Surely she was above this?

Then the elevator lurched, pitching her toward him. Her arm bumped his side and her nose nearly ended up in the middle of his chest. Fizzy excitement imploded in her chest, and her hands rose involuntarily to ward him off, somehow found his hands, and felt her fingers lace through his. Cool against warm, large against slender, firm against soft.

"And I think," he continued softly, "just one more touch, one more kiss…"

His lips were just millimeters away now, his breath wafting over her face. The pulse in her throat skittered violently. Her eyes and thought blurred as his face descended, but she was aware enough to know she lifted her chin to meet him. Parted her lips slightly to meet his, just like before.

And when they touched, it was as exhilarating as she remembered, maybe more so because of the absolute taboo of it. Her boss, the public arena, the air of entitlement that emanated from every pore in his body.

He took her lips hard, greedily. Her eyelids fluttered closed and her fingers curled more firmly around his, tugging him closer.

His mouth devoured hers and the heat of his body surged through him into her. She kissed back, absorbing the shock to her system, accepting the danger. The warm slick taste of him exploded through her, mingled with the wine, her want, his primal need. Helplessly trapped in mindless lust, his arms were the only place she wanted to be.

His tongue slid across hers, erotic and intoxicating. She pressed against him, tugging her hand out of his grasp so she could touch him, run her hands up his long, broad back and up over strong shoulders to the skin above his collar.

He slapped one palm on the wall beside her head and leaned into her, pressing all the way down her body. Then his free hand plunged into her hair, tugging at the comb that held it back. She heard a tinny clink as it fell, felt the cool sweep of her hair on her bare shoulders before he bundled up a huge handful of it in his fist and gently coaxed her head back to expose her throat. Then his hot mouth moved down, burning her skin as it tracked her throat, sucking on the frenzied thump-thump of her pulse, lower to the crease between her breasts, where he stilled and inhaled deeply for a moment.

His hands stroked firmly down her back to her bottom. He spread his fingers wide and dug his fingers in, rendering her as weak as a kitten as he pressed her firmly against him. His eyes fierce and hot, he captured her mouth again, and she met him, tongues thrusting, hips grinding and hands tangling in hair.

Just like the first time, she met him all the way.

The elevator dinged.

Three

Reality returned with a crash. In the hum and downward pressure of the car braking, Madeline pulled back jerkily, wrenching her eyes away from him. Unfortunately, as she moved to maneuver around him, she caught the whole grotesque thing on the mirrored wall of the elevator. Lipstick smeared, hair tangled. Somehow the skirt of her cocktail dress seemed hitched high up on thighs that visibly trembled.

Self-disgust and fear of being caught kept her moving. She hurriedly pushed her dress down and then ran a hand through her hair, dragging it down in the forlorn hope that it may look as if it started that way. Lewis bent and retrieved the comb from the floor and handed it to her. She couldn't look at him.

Out of the fry pan and into the fire! She was never going to be able to work with him, precisely because she was never going to be able to resist him. Every time he clicked his fingers, she'd come running.

The door opened on her floor and a young couple got in. Madeline shoved past them, rummaging in her purse for her key. When she heard a step behind her, her heart plummeted even lower. This was his floor, too, since he was staying in the Presidential Suite just down the hall.

She felt him come up behind her, and the keycard wobbled in her hands. She dropped it and had the ignominy for a second time of seeing Lewis Goode retrieving something of hers. *Pick up my fallen pride while you're there,* she thought despairingly.

She held out her hand for the card. Lewis leaned against the wall, looking amused. "Aren't you going to invite me in?"

Wordlessly she shook her head, her arm still stretched out for the keycard. She'd met women who'd fallen from grace in the workplace. They were sad cases, reduced to positions well below their ability because of a lack of respect. Men got away with it, but sleeping around was the death knell for a woman's ambition. And sleeping with the boss was a sure-fire way to get any other female executives in the organization off-side, not just the men.

Lewis lifted his arm, his eyes darkening to forest green with what could be disappointment, and swiped her card through the lock. "I meant what I said. If you resign from Premier at this stage, there will be consequences. The future of these hotels rests on your shoulders."

Madeline put a steadying hand on the door so that it opened a mere inch. "I don't see how we're going to get past this."

Lewis pushed away from the wall and handed her the card. "What we do or don't get up to in private is no one's business but our own. I need you onboard to teach me the hotel industry. From what I've seen and heard, the operation in this town is in trouble. You can attempt to persuade me otherwise, or your friend and ex-neighbors can look for another employer. Closing these three unprofitable hotels would free up a lot of cash to put towards the new head office in Sydney."

"Sleep with you or everyone gets the chop? Is that it?"

"No. Sleeping with me is optional and should be done because you want to. Resign and everyone gets the chop."

The elevator dinged again, and Madeline pushed the heavy door to her suite open and rushed in. She sagged against the door, breathing heavily. He'd laid it on the line. The choice was hers. And what a choice.

* * *

The next morning she had a headache for real as a consequence of how little sleep she'd had in days. As galling as it was, she peeked through the peephole before exiting her room and took the stairs instead of the lift. The memory of herself in the mirrored wall of the elevator was a great motivator for exercise.

Her mother liked to nap in the afternoons, so Madeline generally visited during the mornings and evenings. Often she found her watching television, something Madeline was rarely allowed to do when growing up for fear of being corrupted. The Alzheimer's disease had taken years to set in, but now it seemed that with every visit, her mother was less cognizant and often did not recognize her.

Today she patted Madeline's sleeve, sniffing about her "fancy threads."

"Plain cooking, plain clothes, plain hard work," was an oft-repeated phrase in the Holland house. Tasteless food and drab, shapeless clothes colored Madeline's recollections. But it hadn't always been like that.

"You used to have a dress this color." She took her mother's leathery hand and placed it on the arm of her midnight-blue sweater. "I remember you and Dad took me somewhere, and how pretty you looked."

Her mother's face smoothed out a little in wistful remembrance. "We went to a wedding dance. The Robinsons'. You were five."

"You and Dad danced."

Her mother blinked several times, a faraway look glistening in her rheumy old eyes. Madeline's heart swelled and she felt a girlish certainty that she hadn't dreamed the good times. She'd been the apple of her parents' eyes until her father had died.

"They divorced, you know," her mother muttered, her face lapsing into its customary censure, thin lips pressed together. "Who didn't see that coming? Their wedding was the only time they ever entered the house of God."

Madeline sighed. It hadn't been all bad, but the reminiscences were few and far between—and of short duration.

"Get me my spinning wheel, Nurse," Mrs. Holland ordered, peering at her tetchily. "Idle hands…"

She had a nasty cold, and soon succumbed to a violent coughing fit that racked her small frame, and Madeline sat her up, patting her on the back. For the first time, her mother seemed fragile. Had she lost weight?

"Has the doctor been today?" she asked the nurse after half an hour of unsuccessfully persuading her mother to have a cup of tea. "She doesn't look good at all."

"The doctor does his rounds tomorrow," the nurse told her. "We'll keep a close eye on her, and if her temperature rises or there is any change, we'll call the doctor."

"And me," Madeline said firmly, checking that they had her cell phone number.

Next she drove out to her family farm on the outskirts of town. She had finally chosen a real estate agent to market the property. A lot of the big stuff had been disposed of last weekend in a garage sale. Now she had to finish packing her mother's clothes and personal effects and clean the place from top to bottom before it could officially go on the market.

Clearly, from the state of the house and the grounds, her mother had not been coping for some time to keep on top of the maintenance. Feeling uncharacteristically nostalgic, Madeline wandered the house and the surrounding outbuildings. Much of the land had been sold off when her father died over twenty years ago, the victim of a freakish farm accident.

Her poor mother, out here all alone while the house crumbled around her. What sort of a daughter was she? She sat on the window sill of her old room, looking out at one of the most stunning vistas she had ever seen, and she had seen a few.

Madeline was a late child, her parents well into their forties when she was born. If only she'd been a boy, or had the slightest interest in taking over the running of the farm that had been passed down from her great-grandfather.

But after her father died, her mother's pious disapproval of and disappointment in her daughter seeped into every corner of the house. Madeline dreamed of escape and freedom from the time she hit puberty.

Her cell phone rang and she answered it on the first ring, thinking of her mother and her poor cough.

"Madeline?" the deep male voice said while she tried to identify the number. "Lewis. Kay gave me your number. Where are you?"

The peace and nostalgia she'd gathered shattered. "At my mother's house."

"There is a workshop I want you to attend in Meeting Room Three in twenty minutes. Be here."

He hung up.

Madeline slid off the window sill, cursing softly. Who the devil did he think he was? She was on holiday, dammit. Checking her watch, she ran out to the car, muttering about his peremptory tone and unfair expectations, but years of professionalism triumphed. She'd changed from her jeans and walked into that meeting only one minute late.

Lewis's head rose and he tracked her all the way to her seat. Ignoring him, she looked at the information screen at the front of the room.

A symposium on eco-waste in the hotel industry? Concealing her irritation, she compressed her lips together and hoped she wouldn't doze off. It was bad enough she was here when she hadn't even officially started work yet, but he could have chosen something a little more scintillating.

For the next hour she listened, fuming inwardly. But suddenly Lewis turned to her. "Madeline, our COO, has managed many hotels overseas. Perhaps she could enlighten us on how other countries manage their waste."

Her heart skipped a beat, but she somehow managed to cover her dismay. "I have nothing prepared."

"Wing it," he suggested.

Madeline pursed her lips, trying to see past the benign gaze to what lurked in his mind. Was he testing her? Perhaps he wanted her to fail.

Madeline would not let him win. She rose, cleared her throat, and spoke for ten minutes, and it wasn't until she took her seat again, to a smattering of polite applause, that she felt the sweat cooling on her back.

At the end of the session, she rose to follow the others out of the room, but Lewis raised his head and his brows, halting her. She reluctantly slid back down into her seat.

"Well done," he said simply when they were alone.

Madeline exhaled, thinking she deserved more than that. "Was that a test?"

He shrugged. "A test?" His lips pursed thoughtfully. "Or punishment for bunking off today?" Then he rested his chin on his hands and looked at her intently. "Or maybe I was just bored and wanted something nice to look at."

Madeline swallowed her swelling temper. "As you know, I'm not due to start till the first of next month.

I need to be excused from the conference to make arrangements for my move to Sydney."

Lewis turned away from her as if he was bored and snibbed his briefcase. "There are four more days of conference left and as my COO, I expect you to attend all relevant workshops and activities. You will still have two weeks to make your arrangements when the conference closes."

She inhaled carefully. Anger nibbled at the edges of her control, but she could do this. She'd earned her position and was the consummate professional. He wanted a reaction? She wouldn't give him the satisfaction.

If Lewis was disappointed with her lack of response, he didn't show it. He glanced at his watch and stood.

"Come on, we don't want to miss the—" he peered at the program in his hand "—Things Get Personnel lecture in the auditorium."

"I have an appointment this afternoon." She was supposed to meet the real estate agent at the farm in an hour.

"Reschedule," he told her and then he smiled at her. The warmth of it hit her right in the solar plexus. Pure pleasure curled her toes, and her own lips twitched. She remembered that smile from their illicit night together. He hadn't been so stingy with his smiles that night.

"I love HR people, don't you?" he asked, still grinning. "Things Get Personnel…" He walked out ahead of her, chuckling, while she gathered her things and followed, hiding her own reluctant smile.

The next three days passed in a blur as Lewis insisted she attend every workshop, meeting and cocktail function going, as well as the team-bonding activities Kay had organized. Madeline may have been brought up here, but she'd never tried any of the myriad adventure activities on offer, although she had learned to ski passably in Europe.

They jet-boated the Shotover River, twisting and turning through frighteningly narrow canyons. There was skiing and luging and one crazy moment where she mentally said goodbye to the world as she was strapped into a flimsy chest and seat harness and swung out over a gaping canyon a hundred meters up, screaming her head off at 150 kilometers an hour.

She accepted every dare, every challenge because that's what she'd learned you had to do to get ahead. She may not have been the most proficient skier or the fastest on the luge, but she would die rather than let her colleagues see her back down. Especially Lewis. Perhaps because of the way they started, she wanted his respect, first and foremost.

And darn it, it was fun!

But all this activity was exhausting. She spent her evenings rushing from cocktail functions to visits with her mother, who was still bedridden with a cold, and to the farm to pack and clean. To save time, or perhaps to avoid running into Lewis outside conference activities, she spent some nights at the farm in her old room, but retained her hotel suite.

Finally the last day of the conference dawned. She dressed warmly for the programmed tandem skydiving, but Lewis announced that he would treat four volunteers to a helicopter ride to the West Coast for a spot of underground caving.

Madeline was pretty sure she'd prefer the wide-open sky to crawling around in dank, dark caves. But Lewis's eyes swiveled straight to her while several other executives vied for the opportunity. The challenge glowed in his eyes and so, against her better judgment, she joined the group.

It started off so well. The helicopter ride was fantastic, and the 130-meter abseil down into the cave presented no problems. Once underground, they used wire ladders to access rifts and waterfalls, but after only half an hour, Madeline felt a deathly fear looming up on her in the darkness. She didn't think anything could surpass the fear of the canyon swing yesterday, but she was wrong.

She began to sweat, a cold sweat that trickled down her back and slicked the chin strap of her helmet. Her chest constricted like a crushing weight. Every step was torture and she began to lag, just a few steps behind the others, but not far enough that she couldn't see them. What was happening to her? The walls of the cave and the dark pressed in on her until her vision diminished to a tiny white spot ahead of her.

She couldn't lose it now, could she? Fighting down a numbing panic, she concentrated on just putting one foot in front of the other, as they squeezed through tiny spaces, navigated waterfalls. It was a nightmare Madeline could not wake up from. She was drenched in cold clammy breath-stealing panic.

Suddenly Lewis's voice filtered through her, calm and reassuring. "You're all right. Take some deep breaths." He loosened her chin strap.

She tried to breathe, but sweat poured down her face, and she felt a scream start to wind its way up from her chest.

Lewis slipped his arm around her shoulder and gave her a brief hug. "I'll get you out. Wait here just a minute." He jogged ahead and spoke briefly to the guide. Madeline felt so afraid and so sick that she wasn't even embarrassed at showing herself up. Then Lewis was back, guiding her out of the loathsome hole, holding her hands when space allowed, all the while talking in low, soothing tones.

Finally they were out in the fresh air and Madeline tore her helmet off and turned her face up to the weak winter sun. Lewis pulled her down to the ground and pushed her head down between her knees, ordering her to breathe.

Furious, but relieved that her breathing was finally calming and a little color returned to her deathly pale face, Lewis kept pushing her head down between her drawn-up knees.

"What did you tell the guide and the others?" she asked, wiping her face.

"I said you'd sprained your ankle," he said tersely. "Why the hell didn't you say you were afraid? Christ, are you so concerned with your precious reputation, you'd risk your life just so no one will think you're scared?"

Madeline blinked at him. "I didn't know. I've never been caving before."

Lewis hesitated, remembering she had admitted as much in the helicopter. "Well, what is it then? Are you afraid of the dark? Confined spaces?"

She shook her head, looking confused. "No, but I can't remember ever being in both at the same time." She covered her face, still trembling. "Please, Lewis, I'm sorry I ruined your trip, just go back and leave me alone. I'm fine now."

"You're not fine," Lewis said gruffly. "Look at you, shaking like a leaf, drenched in sweat."

And yet, still so appealing, he thought wryly. What a sicko he was.

She fumbled with the domes of her overalls. Lewis reached forward and tapped her hands away, popping the domes himself. "The guide said there's a first-aid kit in the truck. I suppose I'd better bandage you up, since you'd die if anyone knew you're not perfect."

He went to the car for the kit, leaving her to scramble

out of the overalls. Why had he pushed her so hard? He knew she was competitive, would never back down from a challenge. Hell, he'd known that from day one.

Madeline sat stiffly while he bandaged her fake sprained ankle for the benefit of her pride. She was pale and subdued on the flight back to Queenstown. Did she really think Lewis gave a damn about one small phobia? That anyone would give a damn? She was flesh and blood, not a superwoman.

"Meet me at ten tomorrow outside the Waterfront."

She halted on her way across the car park, dark shadows under her eyes. "The conference is over. Aren't you going home?"

"I have one last job for you." A job that would test her loyalty. At least, that was the excuse he gave himself. But wasn't it really because he just wanted to spend more time with her?

Lewis was relieved to see she looked fully recovered from her ordeal the next morning, and as vibrant and beautiful as ever.

"Get in," he said, opening the door of his rental. "We're touring the Mountain View and Lakefront Hotels."

Madeline stared at him over the roof of the car. "Is Kay coming?"

Lewis shook his head and got into the car.

"Shouldn't we at least inform her?" she asked, worry tinting her voice.

"I'm meeting with her at one to go over the financial situation." Lewis pulled out of the car park. "I want to see the hotels through your experienced eyes. Are they a quick fix or a hopeless cause?"

"Can't I at least warn her? I feel disloyal, both as her COO and as her friend."

Lewis parked at the Premier Mountainview Hotel, shut off the ignition and faced her. "You are about to take over the running of 150 hotels," he told her sternly. "Have you got what it takes, Madeline?"

Her head rose sharply and she turned in her seat to face him. "Yes," she said firmly.

He thought so, too. "Good enough." He snapped off a nod, pleased with her. "Shall we get started?"

Lewis had been so busy enjoying himself, watching her rise to anything he could throw at her, he'd neglected his responsibilities. Yes, he probably was breaking with etiquette not pre-warning the regional manager of an inspection, but he wanted to see where his COO's loyalty and responsibility lay. His knowledge of the business was sketchy enough without wondering if he could trust her.

They spent an hour at the Premier Mountainview Hotel. By the time they left, his mood was as grey as the flaking paint on the wall that ran around the building. The hotel had worryingly low occupancy, worn facilities and a cleanliness issue, although the building was so poorly maintained that it was difficult to define dirt on the cracked and crumbling surfaces. He had a spirited conversation with the manager about the elevators' expired warrant of fitness. As they left, a backpacker bus pulled up and people began alighting.

"About all it's good for," Lewis snarled.

They drove on to the Lakefront. "We'll lunch there," he decided. "I don't know that I have the stomach for any more substandard rooms and bathrooms."

"You have to remember," Madeline cajoled as they studied an uninspiring menu, "Kay only took over fourteen months ago, and her first job was to completely overhaul the Waterfront—a necessity because the conference had been awarded there."

"Premier is four star and above," Lewis told her. "No way in hell either of these qualify." He stared around at the nearly empty restaurant.

"We're early for lunch," she said, following his gaze.

"Or everyone knows something we don't." He leaned back and fixed the waitress with a stare. "May we have some water, please?"

Madeline raised her brows.

"We sat down seven minutes ago," he told her curtly, looking at his watch. "What do you think of the menu?"

She skimmed the cheaply laminated card, grimacing as her finger wiped over something sticky. "A little—tired."

"Bloody comatose."

"Lewis, you referred to mismanagement on a grand scale at the Gala Ball." Madeline leaned forward earnestly. "Kay's predecessor blew his entire maintenance budget on schmoozing important people in the bid for the annual conference, and then splashed out on a whole new troop of courtesy vehicles."

"I'm also aware," Lewis interrupted, "that Kay was manager of the Waterfront at the time. She should have reported it."

Madeline's smile was loaded with cynicism. "I never met Jacques, but I do know the hotel industry. It's the old-boy network, nothing to do with talent or accountability. Reporting him would have killed Kay's career stone dead."

The waitress arrived with water and took their orders.

"Kay had to make a decision," Madeline continued when she'd gone. "She had no choice about the conference, it had already been awarded. So she threw what little she had left into refurbishing the Waterfront."

Lewis had some sympathy. He liked Kay and he was impressed with the Waterfront. Rooms, restaurants, service and conference facilities were world class. But then, he was a novice in the hotel industry.

The food came and, as he expected, it was mediocre in the extreme.

"You have a good rep in this industry," he told her. "Tough, but fair, capable, motivating. We have a lot of work to do because change has to start from the top."

He picked up his fork, looked at his plate and put his fork down again.

"What do you think?" he asked Madeline.

She pushed some limp salad around her plate. "Not great."

Lewis called the waitress over again. "Would you take us to meet the chef, please?"

Twenty minutes later they were back in the car and heading for the Waterfront Hotel. He'd had a few choice words for the chef, who looked as if he would enjoy taking a meat cleaver to Lewis's head, but Madeline had smoothed things over, telling the man she'd gone to school with his daughter.

It took quite a lot to rattle Madeline Holland, he thought admiringly. In fact, he'd only seen her truly rattled once—apart from the caving incident. And he blamed himself there for pushing her too hard.

Whereas rattling her in the elevator had been all pleasure.

They walked into the lobby, and Madeline turned toward Kay's office, but Lewis led her to the elevator.

"One last little job," he said as the doors closed behind them. "The Presidential Suite here. Have you seen it?"

She shook her head.

"It's supposed to be the best there is in all of Premier's suites."

"I'm sure it is," Madeline murmured. "Everything Kay's done here at the Waterfront has been top quality."

"Nevertheless, I'd like your professional assessment."

She nodded and Lewis pressed the button for the top floor. "I have very fond memories of this elevator," he commented lightly as they began to move.

Madeline pursed her lips and looked at him coolly. But then somehow their eyes tangled in memory of hot mouths and busy hands and the silky feel of the skin on her bare arms. He watched her swallow, careful and controlled, almost imperceptible. They carried on in silence, but neither of them looked away.

Lewis unlocked his door, stood back and gestured for her to precede him. But he stopped her in the doorway, dropping his hands lightly on her shoulders. "First impressions?" he murmured, watching his breath lift a strand of her hair.

She jerked forward a step or two. "Uh, light and airy. Spacious." She walked fully into the living area, seemingly gathering threads of composure as she settled into her work.

"The drapery is nice, rich but understated, furnishings elegant and fresh." She turned, looking at the small kitchenette. "First-class appliances—clean. Well-stocked mini-bar. The freezer could use some attention." She walked around the suite, ticking off boxes in her head, dragging it out until there was nothing left, but to go through to the bedroom.

Lewis was hardly listening, standing back and

watching her lips move, but too steeped in admiration to take note. And anyway, he already knew that the suite was impressive.

She was impressive. These last few days, she'd filled all the spaces of his mind, every waking moment. Her skin was like cocoa butter, rich and creamy with a golden luminescence. Ever since the skiing trip a couple of days ago, when she'd worn a pure-white ski jacket, he'd had this burning desire to see her in white again, the contrast between that and her golden skin and intense blue eyes.

"Bathroom?" She turned, jolting him back to the present.

"Through the bedroom."

Lewis wondered five minutes later how long one could wax lyrical about a bathroom's finer points, but he sensed a reluctance for her to move on to the bedroom.

That feeling was certainly not reciprocated. Every cell in his body was on high alert. Enclosed in this suite, he wanted her with more intensity than he'd ever experienced. He'd sorely neglected his love life lately, but the instant he laid eyes on Madeline Holland, his love life had re-established itself in his mind rather insistently. Their one night together had only intensified the ache of desire.

She turned and almost ran into him as he crowded the doorway. Lewis stepped back to let her pass, and their eyes met and hers skittered away, but not before he saw the awareness in their blue depths, the tension in her smooth jaw.

"The bedroom," Madeline sighed.

Furniture…Manchester…wardrobe…check, check, check. She rattled off the amenities like a shopping list and at a gallop, and he smiled because he knew he could affect her this way.

"You know, these are some of the best refurbishments I've seen anywhere," she gabbled, moving toward the door. She paused. "Wow, great entertainment center."

Lewis chuckled. "I never could understand the need for television in bed. I'm either asleep or—I'm not."

Madeline blushed but raised her chin and looked him straight in the eye. "Won't you be late for your appointment with Kay?"

He saw her out and came to a decision that had been skirting around his mind for days. He would have Madeline Holland again or he'd never get her out of his system. He had to know if that one perfect night was a one-off or if they could recreate it. One last night, he reasoned, to prove it was just sex, and then they could both get on with their jobs and their lives.

Four

It seemed every time she ventured into town, someone recognized her and stopped to talk. Madeline had just decided she didn't know the woman in front of her in the supermarket queue, but then she turned and smiled. It was her English teacher from high school.

The woman asked after her mother and then suggested Madeline give a talk to the pupils on career paths. "It's always nice to see one of ours doing so well for herself."

Madeline's heart squeezed in pleasure. That was the second invitation this week. The president of the Queenstown Women in Business Association had called a few days ago to ask her to speak at their next meeting on how to succeed in the corporate world. Madeline had a sneaking suspicion Kay might have put her up to it, but she couldn't help being pleased.

Motivational speaking was something she enjoyed immensely and was lucky enough to be asked to do, two or three times a year. These small overtures warmed her heart, given they were made by people who hadn't seen her in years and probably never thought she would amount to much.

"What do you think of your new boss?"

Madeline smiled. The million-dollar question.

That was another thing the people of this town seemed obsessed by. Lewis had ruffled quite a few feathers with all his talk of change and impromptu hotel inspections. "I haven't had a lot to do with him so far," she told her ex-teacher. "I don't actually take up the position for a few weeks."

"People say he doesn't have the best interests of the town at heart."

Kay had mentioned the hotel-staff tearooms were abuzz with rumors about the threat of closures and redundancies. It seemed everyone knew someone or had a relative working at one or the other of the hotels. It would be a pity if the locals felt the same reserve toward her just because of who she worked for.

She said her goodbyes and was loading her groceries into the car when her cell phone rang.

It was the man himself, asking her to meet him at the new Ice Bar in town. She decided to walk, grumbling to herself that the conference was over and he had no right to any more of her time. But her step quickened, as did her pulse at the thought of seeing him again.

An attendant handed her a fur-hooded parka and gloves, told her there was a time limit of thirty minutes and a drink limit of three cocktails, the first of which was complimentary in the price of the entry fee.

The bar itself took her breath away, and not only because of the freezing temperature. She walked into a huge cavern where everything was made of ice. Walls, the bar, high tables and stools, even a sofa made of ice and covered in animal skins. Candles and a stunning ice chandelier supplied the lighting. At three in the afternoon, it was surprisingly low-key, but because everyone wore the same ice garb, it took a minute to track Lewis down. He sat in a corner, contemplating the wall while tapping a pen on the icy counter top.

Madeline held back for a moment before he registered her presence. She sipped her cocktail through a straw and wondered what he was thinking about. Her primary concern was his meeting with Kay, but beneath the layers of cold air and the clean taste of the vodka warming her belly, a hollow feeling stirred. This may be the last time she'd see him until she arrived at the Sydney office.

Something inside her wanted more than that, even just a final acknowledgment of the night they'd shared. Since then, he'd infuriated her, tested her, and for the last few days, showed signs that he respected her. But maybe their night together meant little to him. Another night, another executive warming his bed.

Lewis looked up and saw her and she stepped forward, putting all her fanciful thoughts to the back of her mind. "Only you would hold a business meeting in minus five degrees."

He raised his chin and met her gaze. "The conference is over. You and I are on holiday."

Madeline decided not to remind him she was supposed to have been on holiday the whole of the last week.

She slid onto the stool beside him. "How was your meeting with Kay?"

"Ominous," he said, folding his arms. "But I didn't ask you here to talk business."

"You didn't?" Suddenly nervous, she shifted and the glass nearly dropped out of her gloved hand. She righted it, but when she glanced at Lewis's face, she nearly spilled it again. She was at the sharp end of a gaze spiked with intensity and began to feel far too warm in the current environment.

"I want you, Madeline," he told her gravely. "Tonight. One last night."

She gaped at him and through a rising swell of excitement and dismay, she didn't even try to interpret his words any other way than as he meant them.

Correction. Than she *thought* he meant them.

He continued to watch her steadily, making no apology or argument for or against his preposterous proposition.

An age passed, but her vocal chords seem to have blanked out in shock. All she managed was a matter-of-fact-sounding "Oh."

Oh. That's nice. Or, *Oh, thanks but no.* Or even *Oh, okay then.* Think, Madeline! How did she feel about this? Excited. Afraid. Scandalized. And yet, hadn't she dreamed of this every single night since the first perfect night?

It was out of the question. He was her boss. "I don't think that's a good idea."

His gaze didn't waver. "Trust me, it's a good idea."

"Why?"

"Because we want to," he said simply.

She repeated his words soundlessly, as if the feel of them on her lips would bring some reality to the situation.

They didn't.

"One last night," he continued, "at the Alpine Fantasy Retreat."

Shoot him down right now, her pragmatic self huffed. Tell him she didn't do interoffice relationships, especially with the boss. What he proposed was crazy, immoral even.

So why wasn't she stalking out of there?

Because she wanted it, too, Madeline realized. One night, just the two of them, that magical setting, and completely secret.

"Did I mention I'm leaving first thing in the morning?"

His smoothly spoken footnote dealt another blow to her resistance. Two whole weeks to worry about how to deal with seeing him again.

How to face her new colleagues if anyone ever found out… "I don't think I can do it," she blurted.

"You did, beautifully, the other night."

"I didn't know who you were, or I would never…Lewis, I've worked hard to get where I am. If this ever got out, I couldn't bear it. I need respect, it's all I've got."

And wasn't that the truth? Madeline lived to work. Without work, and without respect, she was nothing.

"You have my respect and my admiration," Lewis declared without hesitation.

"Tell me this is a test."

He shook his head. "I'm not asking as your boss, I'm asking as a man. And if you say no, I will never hold it against you, I will never mention it again. Although—" his mouth softened "—I won't promise never to hit on you again."

She blew out a long breath, and steam fogged the air between them. "And what if—what if we want more," she asked, "afterward?"

He might be addictive. Imagine if she fell in love! Madeline had never had a broken heart and it wasn't something she thought she would try.

"Do you want more?" he asked politely.

She nearly laughed out loud at his tone. "No," she said politely back.

"Neither do I."

Good. That was settled then. Except she wrestled with a fleeting disappointment that they'd both discounted the notion out of hand, so carelessly and immediately.

"Can you honestly say that you're not tempted?"

She gazed at him, a million thoughts tumbling around her head. Of course she was tempted. That was the whole problem. Who wouldn't be? No strings, no recriminations. No future.

"One night, Madeline. One night to play out all our fantasies and put them to bed forever."

The bleak thought of never touching him again dampened her leaping nerves. She longed to be considering this somewhere in private, away from his knowing eyes.

And did someone mention fantasy?

An illicit night with her wildest fantasy. She picked up her drink with both hands and took a careful sip, buying time. If this was a virtual program with all the choices in the world, she asked herself, what would she choose? A night—no, a week with him at the villa in Greece she'd stayed at two or three times?

She placed the glass carefully back on the counter, knowing there was nothing she'd rather have than what he was offering: a night of passion with Lewis Goode, in a log cabin with a fire, champagne and a big bath.

Madeline teetered on the side of giving in. "You intimated earlier that I was strong," she said, desperate to give herself every reason to turn him down. "If I was, I should be able to reject this—this madness—out of hand."

To Lewis's everlasting credit, no triumph glittered in the depths of his eyes. If there had been, she told herself, she would have walked.

"Isn't it weak to give in to something as trivial as desire when it can only get in the way of our working relationship?"

"Only if we let it." He leaned forward, frowning. "And I reject that what we had last week was trivial. It was much too intense for that."

Madeline almost apologized at his dangerously glinting eyes. She agreed wholeheartedly, and he'd now given her the acknowledgment she'd wished for when she first walked in the door.

Madeline wanted what Lewis wanted, only she was too much of a good girl to say it out loud, to his face.

Then Lewis unwittingly gave Madeline what she wanted. He rose and looked down at her with some seriously nice lights in his eyes, and took one of her gloved hands in his. "I will be at the Alpine Fantasy

Retreat from 6:00 p.m. If you decide not to come, I will look forward to welcoming you to Head Office in two weeks." Then he leaned forward, brushed her cold cheek with his cold mouth and left the bar.

It was Madeline's turn to sit by herself and contemplate the wall of ice in front of her. She was twenty-eight years old. Single. She worked hard, took far too few holidays and lived in hotel rooms. Didn't she deserve the odd departure from her reality?

And the reality was, she was lonely, inhibited, stilted socially and felt rootless. She lacked friends because all her time went on the job, and her success meant that almost everyone she knew looked upon her as their boss.

One night, not long enough to fall in love. Secret, just as she liked it. Of course she was tempted.

And if you say no, I will never mention it again.

Did she trust him on that? Yes, but she could not say exactly why, only that he seemed to be a man of his word. And she'd already trusted him with her body, which was huge for her.

The barman tapped her on the shoulder. "Would you like another drink, ma'am? Your thirty minutes are almost up."

Madeline checked her watch, only three-thirty. What the heck was she going to do until she absolutely couldn't put off the decision any longer?

Six o'clock until "first thing"; maybe twelve hours of illicit sex.

* * *

The text came through when she was on her way to the retreat. *"Cabin 3,"* it said.

Madeline's stomach gurgled uneasily. She had gone to Kay's office, longing to talk, dreading it at the same time. She wanted her friend to say, "Don't be bloody stupid!" And then she could feel justified in sniping that if it hadn't been for Kay's welcome-home-congrats-on-getting-the-job gift of two nights' stay at the Alpine Fantasy Retreat, she wouldn't be flipping out.

But Kay's husband arrived at Kay's office with the twins. Perhaps that forced the decision. Two adorable girls crawling all over her elegant and capable friend, who somehow morphed into a doe-eyed, face-pulling, raspberry-blowing mother, while the girls wreaked havoc on her tidy desk and clothes. Faced with such domestic bliss, Madeline hoped she might recoil from the thought of hours of illicit sex, but the opposite happened. She came away knowing that she unequivocally did not believe her body harbored a biological clock. She was ambitious, wanted the life Lewis did as CEO of a huge company. Like her mother, she did not have a maternal bone in her body.

Madeline was damned if she would throw away twelve years of hard work and study just because she was touched by how chubby and sticky the little girls fingers were on their mother's face and clothes, how soft her friend's eyes were when she looked at her little treasures.

That life wasn't for her. She found a lingerie store and gave her credit card something to worry about, then rushed to her suite and lavished herself in expensive shower creams and lotions.

Now she stood at the door of the cabin, trying not to think about movies she'd seen where the prostitute arrives at a hotel room and knocks on the door. Madeline took a deep breath, opened the door and walked in.

Like last time, colored candles in little glasses sat winking on many surfaces. A cheery fire crackled in the grate and the heavy velvet drapes were drawn. Fresh flowers on a table scented the air, and music played softly on the stereo.

Madeline set her overnight bag down softly on the floor. No sign of Lewis. Was he already in bed? Perhaps drawing a bath?

Turning, she locked the door then started for the bedroom, just as he appeared at the door.

Madeline stopped, barely breathing. Lewis stopped, too, and leaned against the doorjamb, looking as relaxed as she was tense. His eyes washed over her slowly, glinting in the dim candlelight. His hair was slightly damp and swept up over his forehead. The slight cleft in his square chin was accentuated by being clean-shaven. Like their last night together, he wore jeans and a black T-shirt, and no shoes or socks.

He gave a small smile. "My first fantasy fulfilled," he murmured. "You came."

"Did you think I wouldn't?"

"You're no coward." He pushed away from the wall. "Can I take your coat?"

She turned toward the fire, unbuttoning the long camel-colored woolen coat, and handed it to him.

"Champagne?"

Madeline nodded, thinking the bubbles could hold hands with the squillions of bubbles of nerves in her system right now.

Lewis put her coat away, poured two heavy flutes from a bottle in an ice bucket by the table, and came to stand beside her in front of the fire. He held out his glass and touched it gently to hers. "Did you bring a fantasy?"

The pitch of the crystal reverberated through her chest.

Madeline took her time glancing around the room. "It's all here."

Her breath hitched when he reached for her free hand and laced their fingers together. She remembered the little things he did that first night to make her feel liked, respected, a little calmer. Like now, as he kissed the tips of her fingers.

"Would you care to eat in the restaurant tonight?"

She shook her head. They could do room service if necessary, like last time. Now that she'd made the decision, she didn't want to waste a minute on other people, and staying in lessened the chances of anyone she knew seeing them.

Lewis squeezed her hand. "Nervous?"

She inclined her head. "Maybe a little."

"More than last time?"

Madeline nodded again. Now he was her boss and she would have to see him again, maybe on a regular basis. He could make or break her career with one word or sly insinuation. But as she searched his eyes, soaked up the reassurance she saw there, her world became aligned on an axis of peace. It was right to be here.

"What's your fantasy?" she asked breathlessly.

His eyes slid to her lips and he bent his head and closed the distance between them. "I have a few," he whispered, and brushed her mouth with his. "But they all start the same way."

His tongue traced the seam of her lips, coaxing her to open for him, and she closed her eyes. Other than his mouth and his hand holding hers, he didn't touch her. All her focus centered on the silky slide of his lips, the practiced stroke of his tongue, his breath melting into her mouth. So different from the greedy assault in the elevator. All feeling, patient, a leisurely entrée to entice and prepare her for more substantial fare.

A minute later, without thinking, she stretched out her hand to set her glass down somewhere, anywhere, so that she could touch him. Lewis pulled back, took her glass and put both of them on the mantel.

Madeline pressed both hands flat on to his chest, but he circled her wrists and held them away.

"You can't touch," he whispered and bent his head toward her again.

"But I want to…" She gazed hungrily at the tight T-shirt that moulded to smooth muscle, his biceps bulging with tight, smooth skin. She wanted to touch very much, to feel all that tanned, smooth skin under her fingers.

Lewis smiled lazily. "My first fantasy involves me sitting over there—" he jutted his chin toward a chair placed well back in the shadows "—and you right here, taking your clothes off, one piece at a time.

Madeline laughed shakily. "Really? That's it? A peep show?"

His teeth flashed in the dimly lit room. "Oh, that's just the start of it."

He waited while she assimilated that, stroking her cheek with his thumb. Madeline captured the tip of his thumb in her mouth, swirling her tongue over it before releasing it, and watched his eyes darken with desire. "Will you be giving instructions?"

"Most definitely," he said, the hoarse tone of his voice turning her knees to water. Then he walked away to his chair, and when he sat, she couldn't make out his features at all, only his knuckles resting on his knees.

Nervous laughter bubbled dangerously close to the surface. Could she do this, be the woman he thought she was? If Madeline had been told a week ago that she would meet a sexy stranger while on holiday and spend the night making love to him, she might just have believed it. But if anyone said she would knowingly go to a secluded cabin with the express purpose of having sex with her boss, and end up doing a striptease for his gratification, she would have laughed until she cried.

She took a long draught of champagne, pleased about the blow-out on the lingerie. The music he'd chosen was slow and seductive and although she didn't recognize the group, she liked the sound and stood for a minute, learning the beat. Think of it as a test, she counseled herself. But her hand still trembled as she put down her glass. Then she turned to her faceless stranger, put a hand to her blouse and pushed the first tiny mother-of-pearl button through the hole.

Five

"Slowly," Lewis murmured as she stripped the blouse off, revealing an oyster-colored bra that looked luminous in the flickering light. She covered her nerves well, just a slight breathing irregularity, but he already knew that Madeline Holland thrived on challenge and prided herself on her composure.

His eyes drifted over her from top to bottom and his heart gave a thump as it had when she walked in tonight. She'd worn knee-high white boots with killer heels. He couldn't imagine anything hotter.

Her breasts were pert and beautiful, barely dipping when she released the front-opening bra, their rose-tips pointed and aroused. The sight forced him to wet his lips and he pressed down in his seat to stop himself from going to her, filling his hands and his mouth with her. Not yet.

Her hips swayed almost imperceptibly as if the slow beat of the music came from inside her. He watched, mesmerized as she unzipped her skirt and pushed it down, shimmying a little to help its slide. A curse stuck in his throat. A delicate strip of lace hugged her hips with thin straps reaching down to attach to a pair of shimmering stockings. Lewis let his breath whistle out through his lips, trying to recall if he'd ever been with a woman who wore stockings. If he had, she hadn't looked like this.

She reached out with the toe of her boot and nudged the skirt away. The stockings were sheer, paler than the bands of soft golden skin above them. Her long lithe legs glowed in the gossamer sheen of something so wispy and perfect, he could have looked at her all night. Then her hands went to one of the clasps at the top of her leg and he leaned forward abruptly. "No!"

Her head jerked up and she narrowed her eyes in his direction, framed by the light behind her.

"Leave them for now," Lewis murmured, reclining back into the shadows. He wasn't ready to dispense with the most pleasure he'd had in looking at a woman just yet. A sip of champagne to ease his parched throat and he acknowledged the many pleasurable sensations pulsing through his body, his fingertips, nipples, the skin over his kidneys, and his crotch, especially there.

Madeline peered into the air around him then bent to unzip her boots. Again he stopped her. "Not yet."

She straightened, her elegant fingers dropping to her sides. "What now?" she asked, her voice not quite steady.

Lewis leaned forward, his elbows on his knees. "Now I want to look."

Her breasts rose a little as she stood straight, tall, achingly beautiful, a vision in white and creamy lace. He couldn't take his eyes off her. "Tell me you've got nothing on under that—" he waved vaguely toward her "—that lacy thing."

Madeline smiled and brought her hands down to caress the outside of the lacy thing. "Garter belt."

His mouth dried when she slid her index fingers an inch inside the lacy confection and lifted it to reveal a strip of smooth, shimmering satin.

"I'm wearing a thong."

He almost missed her reply, intent on the ripple of her fingers sliding under the fabric. Damn.

"But it's a special thong."

Lewis's eyes shot to her face almost as fast as his heart leapt into his throat.

"It unties," Madeline murmured, "at the sides."

"Does it?" His voice cracked in the middle of the two small words.

Madeline stilled her fingers and wet her lips. "Would you like me to take it off?"

He was a dead man. "That would be—nice."

He sat back into the shadows, squirming to accommodate all the extra flesh and blood straining the seam of his jeans. A deft flick of her wrist here, a flash of silky ribbon there, a firm slide and then her smile as she held aloft a prize to surpass any trophy he had ever desired.

She was killing him. That scrap of material was his to keep if he had to wrestle her for it then drive into town to buy her a replacement.

"I've had a vision of you in my mind for days," he said, rising, tiring suddenly of the distance between them, "but I didn't know then that this—" he opened his palm "—was exactly what I wanted."

Bending, he picked up the bag from a prestigious brand shop that he'd put by his chair, and walked toward her. "Close your eyes."

"Oh, my," she whispered shakily.

"Don't be nervous, it won't hurt a bit."

Madeline obeyed after an apprehensive look at the bag in his hands. Lewis shook out the long snow-white faux-fur coat from the bag, took her hand and placed it on the fabric. Her pink-tipped fingers flexed and then sank into the fur.

She opened her eyes and gasped. Lewis put the coat around her bare shoulders and pulled the portrait collar up so her face was framed in white fur.

"Lewis, it's…"

"Faux fur," he murmured, pulling the sides together at her throat. "I almost wish I'd made reservations at the restaurant, just for the pleasure of watching you wearing this with exactly what you have on underneath."

Madeline looked down at the coat in wonder. "Where did you get it?"

"One of the big hotel shops in town. I didn't have much time, but I knew it was you the moment I saw it."

"You bought this for me?" Her lovely eyes searched his.

Lewis stepped back, holding her hand, and gave her a thorough, smiling inspection.

"Well, for you and for me, I think."

He moved in a couple of steps and bent to kiss her, closing his eyes at the first touch of her lips. His fingers combed through her soft hair, brushing it away from the back of her neck as he pulled her in for a much deeper kiss.

Deeper and deeper, they kissed until they were both breathless, until little claws of impatience raked him, and Lewis needed patience to carry out the rest of his fantasy. Sliding the coat off her shoulders, he laid it on the floor in front of the fire and coaxed her down to lie on top of the fur.

He eased himself down beside her, raised up on one elbow, and looked down the length of her body. Her nipples peaked visibly and he nearly groaned out loud. But not yet, they had all night and he wanted to indulge both of them.

He took her lips again, clamping down on a desire so fierce, he called on all the finesse he could muster. Her response was all and more than he could take. Their tongues tangled in a mating dance until he thought he might embarrass himself on the spot.

He lifted his head, breathing hard. Her lips were plump and moist, but his mouth needed to disperse the pleasure and his hands were growing restless. With his index finger, he traced her chin, circled the hollow of her throat and pressed his lips down gently on her erratic pulse. Down in between her lovely breasts, skirting under and around, squeezing gently as she arched up and into his hands.

Lewis couldn't help it, he just had to taste her again. But as his mouth closed around one taut bud, Madeline's hands sank into his hair.

He raised his head. "No touching."

She inhaled sharply. "But I want…"

"No touching," he repeated. "We're still on my fantasy."

Composure, Ms. Holland. He wanted her screaming by the end of this. She narrowed her eyes but subsided. He watched until her hands fell to her sides, fingers spread wide with the white fur rippling between them.

Lewis bent his head to her breast again. She kept her side of the bargain technically, but there was touching in the way she angled her body up under his caresses and kisses. He lavished his attention on her breasts and the soft flesh of her inner arms, the sensitive dip of her waist. He returned, time and again, to tease her lips. Her body arched high and rubbed against his chest. "Cheat," he murmured and felt her lips curve against his. And he knew he'd never enjoyed a woman so much.

He'd taken her last time without knowing who she was inside. Now he knew some of her, a quick intuitive mind, loyalty, how much she cared about doing a good job. He derived great satisfaction in accepting the trust she brought to their lovemaking tonight. It couldn't have been an easy decision, but trust was probably the thing that swayed it.

He was primed and set to go. His fingers throbbed with pleasure as they slid over her lustrous flesh, her hair, glimmering with shades of honey and cream and gold and spilling over snow-white fur. He tried to focus on the little things before the big picture went up in flames. The sounds she made in her throat when he suckled her, the serrated edge of the straps that joined the lacy confection on her hips to those gossamer stockings, and the lovely band of skin above the stockings, much darker, but just as silky.

He came up again and the scent of her, excited, heated, wanting, washed over him. And all Lewis's good intentions went up in flames when he remembered that there was nothing between him and paradise.

* * *

Minutes hazed into a long block of time that she had no way of measuring because she had nothing to do but succumb to the bliss of his touch. It weighed heavy on her, that she got to just lie there, enjoying herself without responsibility or reciprocation. What had she learned in her meager experience that would persuade him to allow her to touch and give pleasure also.

It blew her mind that he wanted nothing for himself. He wielded his mouth and hands so expertly, building layer after layer of pleasure until she was nearly incoherent with need. Her consciousness cleaved in two, one large part of her taut and trembling and searching for release; the other languid and floating in rapture so warm and safe, she never wanted him to stop. Sex had never been like this before.

It was a balancing act—give in to an aching desire for release or continue to float. She doubted she could have made the decision. He made it for her. A long, slow, gradual pressure, building and layering until his hand, his mouth stopped teasing, showed her he meant business.

His hands and mouth firmed gloriously, his fingers slid unerringly inside to a sweet spot she hadn't known she possessed. Muscles shaking, inside and out, she succumbed to a double whammy of sensation that went on so long the trembling lasted for minutes, that the sound torn from her throat keened in her ears, that her fingers cramped on the soft faux fur of his fantasy, and she wouldn't have been surprised if she'd ripped great clumps of it out.

While she was still only barely conscious, he prized her fingers from the coat, linked hands, slid over her and inside her, and the pleasure was mirrored in his eyes as he looked into her face and sipped at her lips. She still couldn't touch him because her hands were imprisoned in his, but she felt his restraint in the rigid weight of his still-clothed body barely brushing hers, in the fierce grip of his fingers and the taut, veined line of his throat.

He moved slowly, deeply, completely inside her, his thighs pressing the clasps of the stockings she still wore into her flesh. They dug in even more when she lifted her legs to wrap around him, to keep him there. In response, she dug her stiletto heels into the flesh of his back and buttocks. He groaned and lost his smooth rhythm, and Madeline smiled to know she had at least participated to some extent in shattering his control. My, but was she going to get him back!

Later, when she could think straight.

She lifted and angled her hips, in invitation, in demand, and he stilled for a moment. She felt him heavy, pulsing, revving, and then he looked at her again—pure challenge—and they went mad, plunging into each other as though their lives depended on it. They hurtled toward the peak so incredibly fast, the pressure bearing down and overtaking her, roaring, and she crashed over the edge at the precise moment he did. They collapsed in a sweaty, shaking, breath-defying heap.

The sound of their panting drowned out the logs shifting in the fireplace and the low thrumming music from the stereo. Lewis moved the bulk of his weight off her while still managing to be mostly on top. He gently brought her hands down, curled her fingers in his and pressed them to his chest.

It was a long time before either moved. Madeline felt so replete, so heavy with delicious, sated exhaustion, she thought about drifting off, probably did. His weight pressed her into soft fur, caressing her skin in luxury.

She smiled. No man, barring her father, had ever bought her a gift, not a special intimate gift. She'd had a few funny desk calendars from subordinates, but nothing remotely personal, just for her.

Think about that. That was sad.

She shifted. "This probably isn't very good for the coat." *My coat,* even though he'd said it was for both of them.

Lewis grunted.

The CD whirred and shut off. The fire had burned low to sullen embers. It was so quiet, silence coated the air. She turned her head, wondering.

"Listen," she said.

Lewis opened one groggy eye. She smiled at him.

"I think it's snowing."

"You can hear snow?" he mumbled.

"Of course!" She wriggled out from under him and sat up, looking toward the windows. Madeline loved snow. The snows of her childhood were like a gift, at least while her father was alive. They tobogganed down the slope at the back of the house on a sled made of an old car door. An army of two, they pelted her mother when she came out to watch. Later, after he'd gone, she mostly sat inside to watch, but the memories were all good.

She stood and walked to the window, pulling the heavy drapes back. There was an old street lamp across the drive. It was perfect. The flakes drifted down, illuminated in the light, like millions of stars. Her car was lightly coated. She turned around and walked back to the supine man lying on a bed of fur. "Look."

Lewis sat up, still with his T-shirt on and pants down to his knees. He squinted past her out the window. "Is this going to be a serious storm?"

She kneeled in front of him and tugged his jeans the rest of the way down, then turned and sat with her back pressed into his front and he put his arms around her and they watched the snow fall.

"Are you worried about your flight?" she asked. While she would be perfectly content to stay here for as long as it took, she remembered he had an early departure.

She felt his shrug. "I've been snowed in once before."

Madeline leaned back into him and nestled her head in his neck. "Where?"

"Switzerland," he said dourly. "What was supposed to be a dirty weekend turned into four days."

Madeline wouldn't mind four days. "You don't sound as if you particularly enjoyed the experience."

She felt his shoulders rise and fall behind her.

"It was the company, not the snow."

A sharp pang of insecurity bit her. Was it someone in his organization? Was Madeline one day to be gossiped about as a bad dirty weekend, in another cabin with another woman?

"Even CEOs make bad judgment calls sometimes," she said slowly, pushing her maudlin thoughts away. Recriminations were for tomorrow.

"The call wasn't mine," he said shortly. "I was manipulated into the whole thing."

"Do tell." That surprised her, that he would allow himself to be manipulated. Lewis was one of the sharpest men she'd ever met.

Lewis clicked his tongue, rubbing his finger over a small red mark on her upper thigh, a mark made by the clasp of the stockings she still wore. "Her ancient husband was supposed to be there, that's what the invite said. She wanted something, me preferably, or a place for her husband on my board."

"Everyone wants something," Madeline murmured.

"They do," Lewis agreed gravely. "I seem to meet a lot of people, especially women, who want something for nothing."

Her breath hitched. She squirmed around to look at his face. "Lewis, you don't think I…"

"No." He put his finger to her lips. "I asked you, remember?"

Right. Of course he did. "Sounds like you don't have a very high opinion of women," she said, trying to keep it light.

"Present company excepted." He dropped a kiss on the tip of her nose. She turned around again and faced the window, snuggling into his front.

"The needy and greedy seem to gravitate toward me like a magnet," he commented, putting both of his hands down to play with the lacy bands at the tops of her stockings. "That's why I like strong, independent women like you."

She was both—but tonight wasn't about the future. As long as she kept reminding herself of that, she could enjoy the rest of the night and look forward.

The touch of his hands stroking over and under the lip of her stockings reminded her that this was her one night, her perfect fantasy, and it was going to have to keep her warm on all the long lonely nights ahead.

"Lewis." She flexed her legs so that his hands slid up a precious inch or two.

He stilled.

Madeline covered his hands with hers, lacing their

fingers, pressing them into the soft flesh at the top of her inner thighs. "I want something."

She felt his mouth move in a smile on her hair. And an interesting pressure on her lower back. It was her turn, and if she wasn't mistaken, her fantasy was very much up for it.

She twisted around to face him, placing her legs either side of him, and leaned in for a hot wet kiss. Mouths locked, she took the hem of his T-shirt and worked it up, breaking the kiss long enough to whisk it over his head.

He was so beautifully toned, she thought admiringly, finally getting her hands on his smooth, broad chest. She ran her hands over his chest and back and leaned forward to nibble under his ear and down his throat. Lewis scooted forward and she gasped at the ridge of hot steel pressed against her. But when he raised his hands to cup her breasts, she took his wrists firmly and placed them by his sides. "No touching," she said sternly, and a smile turned up the corners of his mouth. "It's my turn now."

She moved down to lave his nipples with her tongue. His breathing became ragged and eyes filled with dark desire. Moving back slightly, she ran her hands down his abdomen and cupped him, watching his chest rise and his eyes glaze over.

"It's my turn," she whispered, rubbing gently, feeling his leap of response all the way to her core. "And now," she said, pushing him slowly until he was on his back and she was straddling him, "you get to just lie there and take it. You're not the boss now, Mr. Goode." To emphasize the point, she filled her hands with him. "I have you in the palm of my hand."

Madeline awoke feeling fantastic, despite having only slept three hours. How was it possible to feel so good on such a miserly amount of sleep?

And then she remembered. This was the Alpine Fantasy Retreat. Again.

She dragged the pillow out from under her head and put it over her face, suddenly hot with adolescent pleasure. What a glorious night. How could she even have contemplated saying no?

If possible, last night was even more perfect than the first. The beautiful coat and all the other things that had made it so special, like chocolate-dipped strawberries and more champagne, and the unexpected snow.

Madeline stretched luxuriously, thinking that if she never lay with another man again as long as she lived, she wouldn't feel cheated.

After another dreamy minute of X-rated reminiscences, she got up and went to face the mess in the bathroom. She knew it was a mess because it had survived a shower and a spell of lovemaking in the spa bath. Madeline the Good tidied up.

Later, making up, she brushed blusher over her cheekbones and the feel of it evoked a vision: Lewis dressed, looking down at her as she lay in bed. She'd heard birdsong, but the room was dark. She'd snuggled lazily down into the feather duvet, her eyes drifting closed, and then she felt the faintest touch of something on her cheek. His hand? His lips? It was probably a dream.

When she stepped out of the bedroom, she saw the white faux-fur coat hanging on the back of the door. She stroked its pristine softness and folded her overcoat up and put it into the shopping bag he'd brought the white coat in. How decadent was that, sneaking out of this den of discretion wearing her lover's fantasy?

Nothing could dim the light in her eyes. She forgot to be tired. She felt so buoyant that not a pang of worry about how she would feel the next time she saw him permeated her rosy glow. The night had delivered total absorption in pleasuring each other, and somehow she knew that it was special to him also and he would never disrespect her or use this against her.

Now it was holiday time. She would spend lots of time with her mother, sort out the farm and house once and for all, maybe even talk Kay into a trip up to Christchurch to see an opera or something.

A great new job, new friends and challenges, the biggest of which would be working with Lewis. And she looked forward to that, too, even knowing how demanding he could be. She would never die of boredom with him at the helm.

Life was great! She turned into the driveway of the farm, smiled at the fog-shrouded trees lining the drive. It was such a beautiful spot, even if it was run-down. Madeline wondered if the real estate agent she'd hired had received any interest yet. There was no rush. She could easily afford her mother's expenses for the time being.

The phone rang as she stepped into the kitchen and tossed her bag down on the table. "What good is a cell phone when you don't have it on?" Kay's voice said.

Madeline sighed guiltily. There was no reception at the cabin so she'd turned the phone off last night. "Sorry."

"Are you alone?"

Foreboding stirred in her gut at her friend's grim tone. "Yes."

Before she could draw breath, Kay went on. "Is your car in the garage?"

"No." Madeline frowned out the window. "Why?"

"I need you to put it in the garage, lock the door and don't answer it to anyone, okay? I'll be there in under an hour."

Madeline sank down onto a chair. "Why? What's happened?"

"And don't answer the phone, either."

"Oh God, is it Mum?"

"No, no," her friend said hastily. Madeline slumped in a chair and heard Kay sigh heavily.

"I don't know how to tell you this, so I'm just going to come out with it."

A sickening pall smothered Madeline's sunny mood.

"I am so sorry, Madeline. Someone from the hotel sold a security tape of you and Lewis in the elevator here on the night of the Gala Ball. You're on the national news."

Six

Madeline swayed in her chair. Someone from the hotel had sold a tape? "Oh my God," she breathed. "Who? Why?"

"I know who," Kay said grimly. "He's sitting outside my office right now, waiting to be given his marching orders."

Madeline closed her eyes. How could this be happening? "Why?"

"My guess is it's a knee-jerk reaction to all Lewis's talk about change." Kay sighed. "People are feeling threatened."

"We didn't even talk about it last night," she realized,

Play the Lucky Hearts Game

and get...

2 FREE BOOKS and
2 FREE MYSTERY GIFTS...
YOURS to KEEP!

Yes!

I have scratched off the silver card. Please send me my *2 FREE BOOKS* and *2 FREE mystery GIFTS* (gifts are worth about $10). I understand that I am under no obligation to purchase any books as explained on the back of this card.

Scratch Here!

then look below to see what your cards get you... *2 Free Books & 2 Free Mystery Gifts!*

326 SDL ESUA   **225 SDL ESXM**

FIRST NAME	LAST NAME

ADDRESS

APT.#   CITY

STATE/PROV.   ZIP/POSTAL CODE   (S-D-07/08)

Twenty-one gets you
2 FREE BOOKS and
2 FREE MYSTERY GIFTS!

Twenty gets you
2 FREE BOOKS!

Nineteen gets you
1 FREE BOOK!

TRY AGAIN!

The Reader Service — Here's how it works:

If offer card is missing write to: The Silhouette Reader Service, 3010 Walden Ave., P.O. Box 1867, Buffalo, NY 14240-1867

BUSINESS REPLY MAIL

FIRST-CLASS MAIL   PERMIT NO. 717   BUFFALO, NY

POSTAGE WILL BE PAID BY ADDRESSEE

SILHOUETTE READER SERVICE
3010 WALDEN AVE
PO BOX 1867
BUFFALO NY 14240-9952

NO POSTAGE
NECESSARY
IF MAILED
IN THE
UNITED STATES

thinking out loud. She'd asked about his meeting with Kay, but he didn't want to talk about business.

"You saw him last night? He checked out of here yesterday."

Her mind churned up with horrible images—she and Lewis groping each other, *that* look on her mother's face…

The person sitting outside Kay's office right this minute… Because of her lusty appetites, someone was going to lose their job. "Yes," she said heavily. "I was with him last night."

She imagined her friend's face in the long, pregnant silence that followed.

"With him," Kay said, adorning her words with the same inflection. "At the farm?"

"At the Alpine Fantasy Retreat," Madeline said. "Where we met last week."

Another five-second pause, then a loud exhalation. "Oh, Christ, Madeline. Another hotel? Did anyone see you?"

"I don't think so."

"Stay there, don't answer the phone or the door, it'll be reporters. Where is Lewis, by the way?"

"Probably in Christchurch, about to leave for Sydney."

"Lucky old Lewis," Kay said dryly. "I'll be out in an hour. Do you need any supplies?"

Madeline was under siege.

* * *

Lewis surprised himself by falling asleep on the plane after an hour's delay in Queenstown while they cleared snow off the runway. He did not wake until the pilot announced their impending arrival into Christchurch Airport. Damn it! He'd missed his connection to Sydney.

Lewis hated changes to plans, but all he could think was—it was worth it. Thirty-four years old and he'd just discovered you could improve on perfection. He thought their first night had surpassed every sexual expectation. He was wrong.

Forget his promises about a strictly working relationship from now on. Lewis was old enough to know that chemistry of this kind was super-rare. Madeline would resist at first. He smiled, knowing what store she put on her professional reputation. Just one of the many things he admired about his new COO.

He disembarked and made his way straight through to the first-class departures counter.

"The next flight to Sydney departs at four-thirty."

Lewis groaned. "What about indirectly?"

"Via Melbourne? In three hours."

There was nothing to do but wait in the Pacific Star VIP lounge. The worst of it was, he could have had another hour in bed with her. As he walked away from the counter, he recalled her face as she slept this morning. He'd stooped and dropped a kiss right on her beauty spot, just like last time. She probably wouldn't even remember.

"Can you make sure I am called in two hours, please?" he asked the hostess on the door of the VIP lounge. "I may try for some shut-eye."

He looked around approvingly. The lounge was very quiet. Helping himself to some juice from the buffet, he chose a comfortable lounger next to a sun-drenched window.

For the first time in his life, he allowed his mind to consider something more than someone to warm his bed occasionally. He pictured Madeline in his old villa in Double Bay. Waking in his bed. Smiling as she ate breakfast on his deck overlooking the ocean. Sitting on his bed rolling gossamer-sheer stockings up her endless, beautiful legs—or better—rolling them down.

They could go into work together…

Whoa, boy! No sense getting ahead of himself. She hadn't even started yet, but one thing was for sure, one or two nights was never going to be enough.

He sat up, suddenly not in the least tired. Things were going to change. It was time he took something for himself now. He would have his COO and her sweet body, too.

Someone tapped his shoulder. "Do you mind if I put the television on?" The man indicated the TV remote on the table beside Lewis. He handed it over, but his inner plasma screen replayed Madeline riding him, still in her garter belt, stockings and boots.

He was going to embarrass himself in public at this rate.

A few feet away, the television chattered quietly, some breakfast TV. He picked up his juice and then heard the word "Queenstown" spoken, saw the light dusting of snow, and then a shot of the Premier Waterfront Hotel.

It was amazing how fond he'd become of the little tourist mecca after only a week....

How would she ever show her face in town again?

With a heart full of trepidation, Madeline turned the television on, knowing she shouldn't, but it was better than restlessly prowling the house while she waited for Kay.

It was worse than she feared. The Alpine Fantasy Retreat had joined the fray now, although the breakfast show host did not mention the name. "An unnamed source has suggested that a top Premier Hotel Group executive and the new CEO, Australian entrepreneur Lewis Goode, have spent more than one night together at a plush Queenstown resort."

Her poor mother. Madeline had put off calling her, hoping that Kay's arrival might bolster her courage. But it was obvious that this story was on the rise.

She called the retirement village and asked to be put through to Mrs. Holland. The manager came on the phone and told her they'd had a couple of calls from reporters and even one from the local TV station wanting to interview her mother. "Adele hasn't had the television on yet. She's taking a nap."

That was unusual, Madeline thought, checking her watch. "Can I rely on your discretion not to talk to any media?"

The manager reassured her. "Of course you can, and we'll make sure no reporter gets near your mother, although I'm afraid we can't stop her watching TV."

Her mother had mellowed a lot over the years, but there were bound to be newshounds in town who remembered her regular tirades. The Bible Lady in full strident flight would make great copy, especially as it would be the second time she'd railed publicly about her daughter.

TV, radio talkback, newspapers—it was everywhere. The Internet had posted the whole shameful tape from the elevator. The camera sat high in the corner and the images were grainy but infinitely recognizable. Her hair hung down her back, her boobs from that angle looking like they were spilling over the low-cut bodice and practically waving at the camera. Lewis's hand had lifted one of her legs so that her skirt rode high and you could almost believe they were doing it. At one part of the show, he appeared to suckle her breast, and she knew he hadn't done that, it was just the angle. But these were the shots the papers would blow up and publish. Worst of all were the two close-up inserts of their faces as they devoured each other, slack-mouthed in lust, their tongues so very obviously tickling each other's tonsils.

She wanted to die. When Kay got there, Madeline threw herself into her arms in a rare foray into self-pity.

"*How* is this news?" she demanded of her friend.

Kay stroked her hair. "Lewis is always big news in Australia, and he's big news here right now because of the perceived threat to the town's economy if he closes the hotels."

"My poor mother," Madeline moaned against her friend's chest as she held her. "It'll be the last nail in my coffin, as far as she and I are concerned."

"It won't. She'll give you hell for an hour and have forgotten it by teatime. You know, if this video was taken in an elevator in Sydney, the whole thing would have blown over by tomorrow. But in your home town, with your history and your mother and the worry about the hotels, they're going to get some mileage out of it."

Madeline wiped her eyes. "I suppose I can forget the Women in Business meeting, and don't even think about the high school."

Kay squeezed her hands sympathetically. "Jeez, Madeline, I've never seen you cry."

Madeline couldn't remember crying, ever.

Their eyes drifted to the front page of the local paper. "You would have to go for a man with his surname." Both she and Madeline laughed shakily at the headline: Madeline the Good has Goode Time in Queenstown.

Kay sobered and fixed her with her best school-marm look. "Do you like him?"

Madeline looked down at the picture in the paper, at the tilt of his head as he kissed her. "It doesn't matter. It happened and it's over and even this morning, I was looking forward to working with him." She wrapped her arms around herself, remembering the warmth and softness of the coat. "Good old-fashioned lust, that's all." She looked up at her friend's face. "It was your fault. We met at that retreat hotel last week. In fact, it was all so perfect, I even wondered at the time whether he was part of the package."

Kay grinned and got up to bring the coffeepot to the table. "I do give the best presents," she said smugly, topping up Madeline's cup. "Tell me everything. I probably can't help, but it will give me a licentious thrill."

Madeline wondered why she hadn't told her before, and if she should be telling her subordinate—Lewis's subordinate. But it wasn't like she ran to her with every failed love affair. There hadn't been any failed love affairs to talk about.

"Have you been there? There is a tiny theatre where guests can book to watch their favorite movie, and they have someone on the door to see you're not disturbed. Around lunchtime on the second day, I watched *Out of Africa...*" Kay nodded approvingly, as they'd both seen it many times.

"Afterward I went for a long walk, then I realized I'd left my cabin key in the theatre. I went back and there was a movie on, but no usher at the door. I peeked in and saw a man sitting in front of the seat I'd used. I figured I could grab my key without bothering him," she explained. It had seemed entirely plausible at the time.

"What was he watching?" Kay asked.

Madeline shrugged. "Some old war flick. Anyway, I'd just put my hand on the key when he turned and grabbed me like that." She shot her arm out and grasped Kay's wrist firmly. "I got such a shock, I yelled out, and then the lights came on and the attendant rushed in, apologizing over and over. But—" she shook her head in wonder "—all I know is, we couldn't stop looking at each other."

Looking into Lewis's face that first time was like being tied to the tracks in front of a runaway train. "I knew I should run, but I just couldn't."

Kay sat back and exhaled, her eyes thoughtful. "And neither of you knew who the other was?"

Madeline shook her head. That still rankled a little, although Lewis had explained that he had no idea she was going to be at that meeting, which seemed plausible since she wasn't on the Executive Committee. "He told me at the ball that he thought Jacques had sent me there."

"He told you at the ball?" Kay frowned. "Not before?" Her face cleared. "So you ran out and he followed and he kissed you in the lift and then you carried on where you'd left off?"

"No, not that night. I was so angry with him I sent him away."

Kay gave a forthright look at the photo in the paper.

Madeline sighed. "Okay, I kissed him, but then I came to my senses."

"And last night?"

Last night…it seemed so right at the time and she realized that even now, with all this upset, she still couldn't regret that.

"I couldn't resist," she said simply. "One last night to see if it lived up to the first." She laughed and there was a tinge of bitterness in it. "A virgin until I was twenty-two—do you think I'm making up for lost time?"

Kay smiled grimly. "I just hope the memory will keep you going beyond the crap that's about to descend."

The home phone rang solidly for an hour before she took it off the hook, cursing her mother for not having an answer machine. Kay had urged her not to talk to anyone in the press, hoping the fuss would die down in a couple of days. So when she heard a car pull up and stop outside, she peeped through her bedroom window, and as she couldn't identify the person, she didn't answer the door. That happened three times during the afternoon.

The real estate agent called midafternoon to say he had an offer on the property to present to her. Reluctantly she agreed to see him, even though she felt too ashamed to see anyone. But she couldn't let a serious offer slide, especially now when all she wanted to do was slink out of town, under cover of darkness preferably, just like twelve years ago.

The agent didn't refuse her polite offer of coffee. Madeline had interviewed several candidates before settling on this young man, liking his friendly and genuine manner. Now, whether it was there or not, she imagined an insolent twist to his mouth and sly muddy eyes. Her cheeks burned during the whole encounter.

"It's a very good offer, Ms. Holland," he told her while she tried to concentrate on the paperwork. "A clean contract like this should go through without any problems, although of course you can counter."

The prospective buyer was a development company. Madeline knew what that meant. The old house and farm buildings would be razed and a hotel or maybe some swanky apartments put up.

Her father was born in this house…

The agent smiled smugly, reminding her that these were small-town people with small-town minds. She bent and signed the contract in the places he indicated and hustled him out the door before he'd finished his coffee.

Tonight she would go and make peace with her mother. Please, God, she wasn't having one of her rare lapses of coherence and lucidity. The house was pretty well packed up and she could get a cleaning company to do what she hadn't been able to yet. And then she could slip off to Sydney quietly and in relative anonymity.

Someone banged on the door and she retreated to her bedroom again to check through the window, castigating herself for being so pathetic. All the years of hard work and hard-earned respect for nothing.

The door knocker hammered again.

"Madeline! For Christ's sake! I know you're in there."

Lewis's frustrated voice filtered through her shame. But—he was supposed to be in Sydney, wasn't he?

"I've been knocking for ten minutes," he muttered as she opened the front door a crack.

He pushed past her, looking grim.

"I thought you'd be in Australia by now."

"I saw the news when I got to Christchurch. Jesus, it's freezing in here." He walked to the old coal range stove and opened the door.

The creases on his suit were sharp, making her aware of how rumpled she was in ancient jeans, over-size jersey and woolly socks. She hurriedly ran a hand through her hair. "Why are you here?"

Lewis turned. "Are you all right?"

Madeline turned away and started to fill the kettle, but then banged it down and leaned on the bench. Her throat had filled up.

Lewis came up behind her and put his hands on her shoulders, squeezing firmly. Making her tension ten times worse.

"It's not so bad, is it?" He gently turned her to face him and smiled crookedly. "It's not the first time my name has been linked with a beautiful woman."

"Is that supposed to make me feel better?"

He pulled her over to the table and sat her down. "Sweetheart, it's not the end of the world. When you get to the top, there are always people who want to pull you down. You must know that."

She shook her head. He wasn't the least upset, but he was a man, after all! "You think I make a habit of this sort of thing?" She paused. "It's just another conquest to you, isn't it? How do you expect me to hold my head up here in my home town, face my mother?"

Lewis frowned. "Why do you care so much? You don't live here, haven't for years." His tone softened a little. "As far as your mother's concerned, it's a little embarrassing, perhaps, but the virginal histrionics are a bit over the top. You're a grown woman."

Madeline stood up, twisting her hands together. "You don't know my mother," she said feelingly, and moved back to the bench with no clear purpose, just to get out from under his gaze.

Lewis rested his elbow on the table, staring out the window as if giving her a chance to compose herself.

After a minute he stood up. "You got anything against me putting a match to that fire?"

Madeline sighed distractedly. "I've had reporters knocking all day, I don't want anyone to know I'm here."

He stood up, took his jacket off and rolled up his sleeves. "I don't know about you, but I got no sleep at all last night. How about some coffee, and then you can tell me why a little indiscretion has suddenly catapulted you into Public Enemy Number One."

Madeline did as he asked, relieved in some way after all these hours floundering in self-pity, to be given orders. Strange when she was much more used to giving them.

Could she make him understand why the salacious publicity was ten times worse because of what happened when she was sixteen? Even Kay said she should forget the shame, that no one judged her on it anymore. But that was before she was splashed all over the media now.

They sat down with coffee and the biscuits Kay had brought out.

"My mother's—difficult," she began, "and very well-known around here." If she wanted to make him understand, it was necessary to tell him some of her mother's more endearing traits, like her public tirades, and practically insisting Madeline parade through the town wearing sackcloth and ashes after the church incident. "She wasn't—isn't—cruel, but she didn't care that as a teenager I was embarrassed by her, especially when many of my friends and most of their parents came in for her tongue-lashings at regular intervals."

"You say she has Alzheimer's now? Maybe she won't even take it in."

"I'll go and see her later," Madeline said listlessly.

"Is that why you left home, Queenstown?" he asked, loosening his tie. She gazed at him, wishing she could recapture the mind-and-body-consuming passion they'd shared. What a sad end to what could have been a stupendous memory.

But her selfish pleasure was what had gotten her into trouble in the first place.

"I left home because I burned the old church down."

Lewis munched on a chocolate chip biscuit, his eyes steady on her face.

"Kay and I worked part-time as housemaids at the Premier Waterfront. We were sixteen, both still at school, but years apart socially. I was very sheltered." Try completely socially stunted, she thought ruefully.

But she did have a normal teenager's curiosity and hormones. So when Kay told her that some of the staff were having a party down by the old church, and that Jeff Drury, one of the houseboys, was going to be there, she couldn't stop thinking about it. She had a huge crush on Jeff even though he was four years her senior.

"On the night, I sneaked out of my bedroom window and met Kay at the end of the drive." They'd spent a few minutes in the car putting makeup on in the rearview mirror. Kay had brought some clothes for Madeline to wear since the clothes her mother made on the old foot-pedal sewing machine were hardly the height of fashion. "I'd never tasted alcohol before. I had two rum and cokes and felt great at first. Everyone sort of paired off. The boy, Jeff, started kissing me and somehow we ended up inside the church, alone. And then I suppose the alcohol kicked in and I began to feel sick. There was kissing and touching, but after a while, I didn't want his hands on me anymore and I pulled away and he ripped my blouse—Kay's blouse."

She was so ashamed; the blouse was new and she'd ruined it. Everything began to overwhelm her. The alcohol she'd drunk, desperation to get away from him and guilt at behaving like this in a church with her mother's stance on morality and religion. "I started to struggle and we must have knocked over the candles we'd lit and put on the pulpit. There was this beautiful big tapestry, very old, draped over the pulpit. But we didn't notice at first. He wouldn't let me go."

Panic added to the mix. Jeff had his hand firmly planted in the crotch of her jeans even while she was hitting and pushing at him. "By the time we smelled the smoke, the pulpit leaning against the wall was well alight. There was so much smoke." She looked at Lewis, still surprised by it. "It was terrifying. You don't expect it to be so black. I mean it was dark, but I thought the flames would light everything up.

"I couldn't see a thing. I kept running into walls and falling over and I couldn't breathe. By the time I made it outside, I was nearly hysterical."

She'd thrown up until there was nothing left, to the sound of the church windows breaking and the roaring of the flames. Madeline just knew she was going straight to hell.

"Jeff and the other kids took off. I don't know why I stayed. It wasn't like I could do anything. Even the fire brigade couldn't save it. But I couldn't leave, I was too guilty. Kay stayed, too."

The church was the pride of the town at that time. It was a small, very old wooden church, set in the most picturesque location imaginable on the edge of Lake Wakatipu. It featured in many postcards of the region, and tourists came from everywhere to be married or photographed there.

The townspeople were appalled, but that was nothing compared to her mother's wrath. "We were lucky not to be charged. I think when the cops dropped me off home, in Kay's torn clothes, covered in smoke, stinking of alcohol and vomit, they probably thought I'd be punished enough." She smiled wryly. "They called her the Bible Lady back then."

Lewis leaned forward. "What happened to the other kids?"

Madeline shrugged. "I think most people knew what happened, but the cops dropped it."

Lewis opened the door of the range and shoveled

some more coal in. "I guess that explains what happened in the cave the other day," he said, and walked to the sink to rinse his hands. "Dark confined spaces."

She nodded, considering. "Maybe." It was a pity she hadn't thought about confined spaces in the elevator last week.

He sat back down, drying his hands on a tea towel. "Did she throw you out or did you go voluntarily?"

She smiled. "I couldn't wait to go. She was unbearable." The shame might have faded a lot faster if her mother hadn't insisted on preaching about the error of her own daughter's ways to anyone who would listen. "I'd saved enough to get me to Australia. And that was that."

"Is this the first time you've been home?"

She shook her head. "No, I come home every year or so for a quick visit, but I don't think she's ever forgiven me. She got a lot softer in her old age, but then the Alzheimer's set in."

A sad laugh bubbled up. "You'll think this is funny. I always thought that one day, I'd ride into town and be the golden girl. The triumphant return of the prodigal daughter. I'd make them all sit up and say, 'Well, she started out bad, but look what she's made of herself.'" She sighed. "And now look what I've done."

Lewis made an impatient noise. "Come on, Madeline. So we had a kiss in an elevator. Hell, let's just hope the Alpine Fantasy Retreat doesn't have cameras in the rooms."

She looked at him sharply. "Don't! I can't believe they told. That place is famous for being discreet."

"I gave the manager a piece of my mind, believe me," Lewis told her grimly. "He phoned today to apologize and said he'd see the culprit never works in the hotel business in this town again."

Another person burned by their total absorption in the pursuit of pleasure, Madeline thought. Another person in this town she'd successfully alienated.

Lewis rubbed his eyes wearily. "It'll pass. Get back out there, hold your head high and show them you don't give a damn. That's what I'm going to do."

Madeline wrapped her arms around her middle. "I *do* give a damn." She wondered if he'd been caught with his pants down—figuratively speaking—before.

And that led her to wonder what interest, if any, there was in Australia about this matter. "Have you heard from anyone over there?" she asked, a hollow feeling squirming in her gut. "Has this made the news?"

"Who cares? Madeline, I'm always in the news."

Knowing that didn't help. "I care. I haven't even thought about that." She closed her eyes in anguish. "How am I going to face my new team?"

How could she expect to be taken seriously once that tape was bandied around? She was starting a new job as chief of operations for a multinational company, and she would start with no credibility at all.

"You will," Lewis said firmly. "Because you're better than that."

Easy for him to say. He was a man. Another notch on the bedpost was no skin off his nose. "Respect is paramount to me, probably because of what I've just told you. I'll be a laughingstock."

Lewis sighed impatiently. "There's no room for weakness at the level you're at. They'll chew you up and spit you out."

"I've seen it time and time again," Madeline argued. "It doesn't matter what I achieve in the board-room, or if I survive this humiliation at first. This will be bandied about every time I do something. Every time I get a promotion or apply for a new job or have to make cutbacks. The snide comments behind my back or veiled references to my face. I got there because I screwed the boss and got caught on camera."

Lewis pushed himself up from the chair abruptly. "Toughen up, Madeline," he said sharply. "Get your ass to Sydney or you'll have more than snide comments to worry about. Remember, the fate of the Queenstown hotels rests on your shoulders."

Her mouth dropped open and she stared at him, stunned. That he could still hold this over her, on top of everything else, cut deeply.

He picked up the overcoat he'd tossed on a chair and put it on. Now she had yet another choice to make. If she took up the position in Sydney, she would start with no credibility at all. If she stayed and survived the innuendo and humiliation by the towns-folk, not to mention her mother, she could then be responsible for the axing of many jobs, including her best friend's.

That would kill any chance she might ever have of being accepted in her home town again.

Lewis shoved his hands into his pockets and stared sternly down at her. "I have an appointment. Meet me for dinner in town later."

"No." She shook her head. "Lewis, I…I couldn't face it."

He leaned down until his face was two inches from hers. "You can't face the town and your mother. You can't face your staff in Sydney. Make up your mind, Madeline, because you can't have it both ways." He straightened. "Seven-thirty at the Waterfront in the restaurant."

Lewis checked into the Presidential Suite at the Waterfront, ignoring the stares of the staff. He had an hour to kill before his appointment and spent most of it trying to push Madeline's strained face to the back of his mind.

He refused to let her throw away a stellar career because of some negative and embarrassing publicity and he'd already put a contingency plan into place to that end. But as he showered to shake off the effects of too little sleep, he kept hearing that old familiar voice whispering in his ear.

I could help her, he thought. I could make things better.

He'd always thought that—until two years ago when revenge became his prime motivator. He'd spent his whole life fixing people up and trying to protect them, and he wasn't going there again. That's why Madeline was such a refreshing change, why he wanted her in Sydney. Not to teach him the ropes of the hotel business; he could hire someone for that. But because she didn't want anything from him. She had it together, ruled with her head not her heart.

And then he had come along and kissed her in an elevator. Lewis was responsible for the unhappiness on her face today.

The suite phone rang.

"Mr. Goode, it's the *Queenstown Daily* here. We heard you were back in town."

The small-town grapevine was alive and kicking, he thought savagely. "What do you want?"

"Do you have any comment to make on the story we broke this morning? Did you see it? I could have a copy…"

Lewis cut him off. "Why would I make a comment to you?"

"Well, sir, sometimes it's helpful to put your perspective across in these matters. You're not the most popular man in this part of the country. We can humanize you."

"You don't have a story," Lewis snarled. "You have a photo and that's it, and you want to drag someone's name through the mud."

"We've tried to get hold of Ms. Holland to put her side, but she doesn't seem disposed to take our calls."

Leave her alone! He wanted to yell, but that might make things worse for her. Damn it! He wanted to make things better.

So he wasn't the most popular man in town, hey? Perhaps the reason the security tape ended up at the local rag was down to him. He'd come into this town trumpeting change, hinting at redundancies, ordering reviews, making surprise inspections. These things could probably be absorbed in big cities, but with a big percentage of the town's population working under the Premier umbrella, maybe he should have reined it in a little.

"Perhaps if I met you downstairs for a drink," the man said, "we could chat about your business interests here. That might take the heat off the lady a bit."

Lewis took a deep breath, wondering if he could actually sit across a bar without planting his fist in the man's face.

He was certain Madeline could handle the office gossip, even if she herself wouldn't agree today. But could he do something to help restore her tarnished reputation here and smooth things over with her mother?

Seething about suddenly finding himself in the role of protector for the one woman he admired for her strength, Lewis told the man he'd see him in the bar in five minutes.

Much later, after his appointment in town, he

returned to the bar at the Waterfront to wait for Madeline. Seven-thirty passed, and he felt the first stirring of disappointment and anger that she might not show. Fifteen minutes after that, he was ropable. After what he'd done for her today, against his better judgment, was she about to show her true colors? Not strong enough to be a worthy prize.

He called her cell phone. She picked up immediately.

"You're late," he ground out, not wanting excuses.

"Oh, Lewis."

She sounded like she was surprised to hear from him.

"I'm at the retirement village. My mother is missing."

Seven

Lewis raced to the retirement village and picked out Madeline standing by the entrance, talking to a couple of police. In the distance her face was a pale smudge, abruptly cut off by the dark-colored beanie she wore. Kay stood by her side, clapping her gloved hands together. All eyes swiveled to him as he stepped out of the throng toward them.

The worry in Madeline's eyes arrowed straight through him, but in light of the day's events, he thought it prudent not to take her in her arms.

"She was last seen eating dinner in her room two hours ago," Kay told him. "She wasn't there when they came back to collect her dishes."

"They've checked her clothes," Madeline said in a voice that sounded like the ache of unshed tears. "She only has her nightie and a pair of slippers on."

Lewis cleared his throat to cover the shiver that rattled his bones in the chill winter air. Remnants of last night's snow still lay on the ground.

"Is there anywhere you can think of she might go?" one of the policemen asked. "A friend? A special favorite place?"

Madeline bit her lip and shook her head sadly.

"The farm." An elderly man in a dark hooded oilskin and thick gloves stepped forward. "She might try to go home." The man put out his hand and patted Madeline on the arm. "Hello, love. I haven't seen you since you were a little-un."

Madeline peered at his face. "I'm sorry, I…"

"You won't know me, Brian Cornelius. I'm a longtime friend of your mum's."

A woman dressed in a white uniform nodded briskly. "Brian visits Adele often."

Mr. Cornelius ducked his head. "Well, I visit everyone. Passes the time on a Sunday since my wife passed away."

"What makes you think she'd go back to the farm?" Madeline whispered.

The old man shuffled about, looking embarrassed at being the center of attention. "She missed her home, the view. Missed her daughter and husband." He coughed self-consciously. "Not all of the time, you understand."

"Perhaps you should go back to the farm," Lewis said to Madeline.

She shook her head. "No, I…I feel I should be here."

Even though she hadn't said it, everyone's thoughts turned to just how far the old lady would get in two hours in the freezing night air, barely dressed.

"I'll go," Mr. Cornelius said.

"Would you?" Madeline grasped his hand. "Thank you so much. The key is under the mat, go inside and keep warm. I'll call the home phone if there is any news."

Everyone split up and fanned out all over town. Apparently, Adele Holland had lived here all her life and enjoyed reasonable physical health until the last few days. Lewis felt a pang of guilt for monopolizing all of Madeline's time over the last week when her mother was clearly unwell.

It seemed the whole town turned out to search, and the still night air resonated with calls of Adele Holland's name. But as the hours passed, Madeline's head dropped. Lewis asked her repeatedly if she wouldn't rather go home and wait at the farm, but she told him she'd go mad if she just had to sit and wait.

"So much for being outcast because of a little kiss," he whispered in her ear, staring at what must be a hundred searchers.

She chewed on her bottom lip, looking stricken. "Lewis, I can't get it out of my head. What if…what if she saw us, on TV?"

Damn! He knew what she was going to say, had wondered himself. He grabbed her hands, squeezing tightly. "She's got Alzheimer's disease," he told her firmly. "Anything could have triggered her confusion."

She didn't look convinced. A deep elemental need to comfort her welled up. Lewis didn't care who saw what or that they were the stars of the current society pages. He began to tug her toward him to comfort and warm her. But someone approached and Madeline snatched her hands away, leaving him standing there with his arms outstretched and feeling foolish.

She wouldn't want his comfort, he realized, letting his arms drop to his sides. Madeline would hate to be seen accepting comfort in full public view, especially by the man who'd shown her up to be human.

They searched for three hours in zero degrees and complete darkness before a shout went up and the news spread like wildfire. Adele Holland was safe. She'd been found on one of the freezing back roads that led out of town. Her old friend was right; she was heading for home. If it wasn't for the many searchers that covered every street, every park and every foot of the waterfront, the consequences would have been too terrible to contemplate.

They rushed to the hospital to find she was uninjured but suffering from hypothermia and a suspected chest infection. Kay and Lewis stayed while Madeline sat with her mother in the emergency department, but the old lady did not recognize her or even acknowledge her adventure and soon went to sleep.

It was one in the morning when Lewis took Madeline back to the farm. Adele Holland's old gentleman friend had left after the call to say the search was over, but had lit the range in the kitchen, which took the edge off the chill. Madeline stood in the middle of the kitchen, as tired and emotional as she could ever remember feeling.

"Have you got anything to eat?" Lewis asked, opening a few cupboards.

She shrugged, too tired to be interested in food. Then she glanced guiltily at Lewis, who looked as weary as she felt, only better dressed. He probably hadn't eaten, himself, since she'd stood him up for dinner.

His peremptory command had angered her this afternoon, even through her shame. Madeline had done all he'd asked of her during the conference. She'd attended workshops, balls, even allowed herself to be flung off a cliff into a canyon. To imply that the future of the hotels still rested on her shoulders if she didn't do what he said was the last straw.

While she'd been standing aimlessly in the middle of the kitchen daydreaming, Lewis had left the room. Now he came back in, took her hand and led her into the lounge. He'd lit the fire and now he pushed her down onto the couch. "I'll fix us something to eat."

Relieved to be alone for a minute, Madeline

stared into the fire, so grateful to her old friends and neighbors for their support tonight. Despite everything, it seemed her mother was very fondly regarded in the community.

Touched by their rallying around, Madeline wondered for the first time whether she was doing the right thing by leaving. Not one person had mentioned the scandal tonight, to her face, anyway, but many had said how proud they were of what she'd achieved, and when was she coming home for good, and even how right it was that a Holland was still on the old Holland farm.

Their reserve toward Lewis was evident, but no one actually challenged him, either about the elevator business or his intentions toward the hotels.

Too tired to think straight, she wondered what the legal ramifications of cancelling the deal on the farm were. Maybe she'd call the guy tomorrow. Madeline yawned and leaned back on the couch, the fire warming her face.

Lewis walked in with a plateful of hot buttered toast. "It's only instant soup," he said, setting down the plate and a couple of spoons, "but it'll warm you up."

Madeline watched him walk back into the kitchen, touched at his fussing. See, she told herself, sometimes he could be nice. He'd certainly been a rock of support tonight. How she wanted to know him. Had he ever been married, been in love? Why did he work so hard and what gave him pleasure?

Madeline curled up on the couch, feeling warmer than the fire should get credit for, knowing exactly what gave him pleasure. Had it ever been like that for him before? she wondered dreamily. No one had ever made her feel like he did. Wouldn't it be nice if she'd touched something in this man that no one else had?

Next thing she knew, she was in his arms and he was taking her somewhere cold. She knew it was Lewis; she remembered his smell and the longish hair tickling her face. But this was way too cold to be the Alpine Fantasy Retreat. She tightened her arms around his neck, glad that he was here to warm her up.

He carried her down the hallway and she groggily told him the way. The bedroom was cold. Boxes containing everything she'd loved and left lined one wall. Still holding her, he walked to the single bed and tugged the covers back. Madeline nosed her face into the skin of his neck and inhaled, strangely embarrassed that he was here in her childhood bedroom, nowhere near the luxury he was used to.

His arms tightened and he even brushed her cheek with his lips very briefly as he lowered her to the bed. With fuzzy surprise, she thought she hadn't equated tenderness before from Lewis.

She supposed she hadn't needed to.

Lewis sat on the edge of the bed beside her. "Lift your arms."

She complied and he whisked the jersey she wore over her head, leaving her in a long-sleeved tee. She flopped back onto the bed and he turned and began easing her Ugg boots off.

"I could get to like this gentle side of you," she murmured, not realizing until too late that she'd spoken aloud.

Lewis gave a tight smile and set her boots on the floor. "I've had plenty of practice."

Madeline knotted her brows. "Practice?"

He lifted up momentarily and pulled the covers up to her chin. "My mother was an alcoholic," he said. "I've put her to bed hundreds of times."

Wow! A personal detail. He wasn't big on revealing them. Mind you, neither was she. So his mother was an alcoholic. Questions whispered through her tired mind, but then got stuck on the word *mother.* Lewis's personal history retreated while her mind and heart filled slowly with sadness and relief.

"Lewis, I don't think I can leave my mother," she whispered, snuggling down under the covers and closing her eyes.

He took so long to answer that her thoughts wandered to the dream she'd had where he'd leaned down and kissed her cheek. Sometime, somewhere, long ago. A muted longing for him to do just that drifted in and out of her mind.

"I think you're too tired and emotional to make any decisions now," he murmured as if in her dream. "Get some sleep."

Fine by me, she thought, sighing, *if you're not going to kiss me.*

"Can you tell me where I can find a blanket or two? I'll park up on the couch."

Madeline moved her head vaguely. "Next room," she mumbled. "Boxes."

She was asleep by the time he left the room.

Madeline slept for nine hours.

She walked into the lounge to find blankets neatly folded on the end of the couch, the curtains drawn and no sign of Lewis's car on the drive.

Her mother was comfortable and on the ward, she was told when she called the hospital, but they wanted to keep her in for another day to monitor her chest infection.

Relieved, Madeline unrolled the newspaper Lewis must have brought in from the step with only a little reluctance. Somehow the scandal had taken a backseat in light of yesterday's events.

Lewis and Our Madeline Are an Item! the headlines read. The pragmatic side of her sighed at the fact that this sort of gossip passed as news in the only supposedly serious daily paper in the region.

The personally involved woman in her took a deep breath and read the article.

Mr. Lewis Goode of Pacific Star Airlines and new CEO of Premier Hotel Group has broken his silence on the kiss in the elevator affair, run by this newspaper yesterday.

"Madeline Holland and I are in a relationship of some duration," he says. He had asked the high-ranking corporate executive to move to Australia to be closer to him. He denies knowing that she had applied for and landed the top Chief of Operations position in Premier at the time he concluded his corporate takeover of the massive company here in Queenstown last week. Ms. Holland could not be contacted last night for comment.

In news the local population will be relieved to hear, Mr. Goode intimated that Ms. Holland has personally persuaded him to reconsider his plans to close the three Premier hotels in the town.

Madeline took the article and her coffee to the step to reread it in the sun. "'Madeline Holland and I are in a relationship of some duration.'"

What had prompted him to do that? Could Lewis have feelings for her? The possibilities zinged about her brain. Did he want a relationship "of some duration" with her? Probably he just felt sorry for her about her mother going walkabout—no, he'd have had to put the statement out before that to get it in the morning papers.

Madeline was touched. He'd said it because he

wanted to make her feel better. He knew how ashamed she was about the grotesque tape splashed over the news. She had to admit, it would certainly make her feel better and may even appease her mother.

Her buoyancy lasted all of three minutes. The fact was, there were no facts. It was a great big lie, and that made her uneasy. Lies had to be sustained. Lies had a habit of coming out. The paper—or if not this one, another—would continue to try to contact her for comment. They would ask questions, Where did you meet? How long ago? Questions she had no answers to. What on earth could she say that had a ring of truth to it?

The phone rang and, to her surprise, it was the president of the Women in Business Association, confirming her invitation to speak tomorrow night. Feeling lighter than she had in the last day and a half, she called the real estate agent about the status of the contract she'd signed.

"It's with the lawyers at the moment."

"Say, hypothetically, I change my mind about selling. How would that work?"

The agent told her that only the purchaser could crash the deal at this time. "There would be substantial penalties if you renege on a signed purchase agreement." His voice had a tinge of annoyance about it.

"It was just a query," Madeline said and hung up, her brow furrowing. Damn. She hadn't made a final decision on her future yet, but it was nice to have options. Could she consider staying in Queenstown and not living at the farm?

She raised her head and drank in the glistening lake and bristling mountains above. She didn't think so.

She would just have to pay the penalties, then. She could afford it, if and when she made the decision.

Her mother was at her strident best that afternoon, running everyone ragged.

"Thank the Lord you're here," she said when Madeline walked into the ward. "You have to take me home."

Madeline had already spoken to the staff nurse on duty. Her mother had a fever and they were worried about her cough. She was allergic to strong antibiotics, just another thing Madeline hadn't known about her.

She took her mother's hands and sat down beside the bed. "Mum, you have to stop playing up. You have a chest infection. They need to keep you in here just a little longer and keep you warm."

Her mother seemed comforted by her presence for once. They talked of the farm and dogs they used to have. Madeline thought how old her mother looked. She was old, she supposed, but for the first time she seemed frail. And that was the last word Madeline would ever have used to describe her mother.

"Madeline?" her mother suddenly said in a perfectly calm, lucid tone—a rare occurrence these days. "I have something very important to say to you."

She started guiltily, knowing she was about to get

a right royal telling off, and if she knew her mother, everyone on the ward would hear. So her mother *had* seen the news yesterday.

Madeline was wrong. In fact, she discovered she'd been wrong most of her life:

Her mother had indulged in an affair that spanned several years, but the day she broke it off, realizing that she loved her husband and daughter too much to go on, was the day Madeline's father was killed.

Everyone thought after John Holland died that her mother changed and became the righteous zealot she was out of grief. But it was much more than that.

"Don't you see?" her mother cried. "I never got his forgiveness. That's why I've been so horrible and pushed you away all these years. I was the biggest sinner in God's Kingdom and so I punished everyone else, most of all you."

Madeline reeled with the revelations. When was this emotional roller coaster going to stop? She shushed and tried to placate her poor mother who was beside herself with guilt and shame, apologizing over and over for pushing her own daughter away.

When Madeline finally left the hospital hours later, she could not shake an ominous feeling that they didn't have much time left to forgive each other. For wasn't Madeline as much to blame for letting her mother get away with punishing her? She'd just accepted that that's the way things were and had abandoned her poor mother, when perhaps with a bit of love and understanding they could have forged a closer relationship and her mother could have forgiven herself.

She pulled up the driveway of the farm and saw the lights on, smoke curling out of the chimney. And her decision was made.

Madeline was home.

Eight

Lewis gave up trying to pretend anymore.

Madeline sat opposite him at the kitchen table, disinterestedly pushing the steak and stir-fry he'd made around her plate. She'd just recounted the details of her visit to the hospital and she looked done in. And he'd stopped pretending he didn't want to help anymore.

Lewis knew all about how the actions of a parent impacted a child, shaped their lives. If he was lucky enough to have kids, he would make damn sure any mistakes were owned up to and compensated for at the time, not left until the children were scarred by it.

"Rough day, huh?"

She smiled sadly. "Rough couple of days."

He'd not had a good day himself. The statement he'd given the paper had caused a bit of a fuss amongst the board of directors. From the calls he'd taken, no one had a problem with him sleeping with the newly appointed COO. They did, however, have doubts about a potential conflict of interests. Had Madeline known about the proposed corporate takeover? And how much, if any, influence had Lewis had over her appointment?

With Kay's help, he'd spent the day organizing a telephone conference call with all of the board for tomorrow. Most were en route back to their countries of residence. Only two of the directors lived in New Zealand and he was picking them up from the airport in the morning. There were several in Australia, and some as far afield as Paris and the United States, so time zones had to be considered. He'd finally nailed them down to midday tomorrow. He expected to be hauled over the coals for his actions, but he wasn't sorry. Madeline was blameless. She'd gotten the job on her own merit. No conflict of interest as far as he was concerned.

She finally pushed her plate aside, put her elbows on the table and steepled her fingers. "About the statement you made…"

He didn't regret sticking his neck out for her on this. If they kept to the same tune, he was sure he could sway the directors. "It should, I hope, ease some of your embarrassment here."

"It does, and I'm grateful." She paused. "But it's not true."

"It doesn't obligate you in any way," Lewis said quickly. "It's just a united front until the fuss dies down."

She inhaled. "It obligates me into perpetuating the lie."

Lewis steepled his fingers, mimicking her. "It sounds a bit better than what everyone thinks, that we had a couple too many drinks and decided to have a quickie in a public elevator."

She blinked. "As I said, I am grateful. It was—nice, what you did. But these things have a habit of coming out. People are going to want to know the whens and the wheres. We're digging a hole for ourselves."

But we're in it together, he thought. "Well, I think it will blow over quickly now. And when you get to work and people see you in action…"

She chewed on her bottom lip. "Perhaps my position in the company might be compromised."

Lewis should have known she'd realize how the corporate mind worked. He shrugged. "I've organized a conference call with the board of directors tomorrow, but don't worry about it. I think I can shoot down their concerns."

Her brows arched.

"Conflict-of-interest issue. How much you knew

about the takeover and so on." Something stopped him from citing one of the directors who suggested that perhaps she wasn't COO material. "Leave it to me. There's nothing to worry about, so long as we're on the same page."

"Same page?" she asked.

Lewis sighed patiently. "If anyone asks, we met overseas, I asked you to move to Australia. You knew nothing of the takeover bid, since you'd lived overseas for years and we didn't waste our precious time talking business."

Her brows lifted even higher.

"You kept the Premier job news a secret and came over here to attend the conference and sort out some personal stuff. We'll say it was as much a shock to me to see you in the Executive Committee meeting as it was to you when I walked in." He smiled wryly. "That, at least, is the truth."

Madeline held his gaze steadily. "Sounds like we need a scriptwriter for all that."

That ticked him off. He'd thought he was helping.

"The newspapers are after me to make a comment," Madeline said. "That's an awful lot to lie about. What if they ask for dates and places, where we met, when?"

"Say no comment. They'll get bored soon enough and I'll handle the directors, don't worry about that," he said confidently.

"You wouldn't have to handle the directors if you'd discussed it with me first," she said quietly.

Lewis sat back in his chair and put his hands behind his head. "You've got a lot on your mind."

"It's my mother," she said, looking away from him. "I don't know how much time she has left."

"What do the doctors say?"

"It's not what the doctors say. It's me. I feel I should be here for her now."

Lewis exhaled. "Well, take some leave. A couple of weeks, and then, when she seems stable…"

"I want to make it up to her so at least she doesn't have me on her conscience, as well."

She'd spoken almost over the top of him, as if she hadn't heard him. Now she picked up her utensils and began scraping her leftovers onto his plate.

"Leave that," he snapped. "Take some time…"

"My priorities have changed," she began.

Why was he even bothering? "Use your head, Madeline. What the hell would you do here? You're a businesswoman, not some small-town girl."

She picked up both plates and stood. "I thought so, but…" She turned and walked to the sink.

"Don't you think you're being a bit emotional about this?" he asked.

The plates banged down on the bench with a crack. "She's my mother, for God's sake! I'm allowed to be emotional." Her back bristled with tension and she just stood there at the sink not facing him.

Lewis lost the battle with his patience. "There are

retirement homes in Sydney. I'll get my assistant to send you some information."

Madeline whirled around, eyes flashing. "This is her home. She's lived her whole life here."

Something had changed; he could see that. He'd done his best to needle her throughout the conference, but it was "steady as she goes," all the way.

Not anymore. He took a deep breath. "She has Alzheimer's disease, Madeline. Most of the time she won't know or care where the hell she is."

She jerked as if he'd slapped her. Her eyes filled with disappointment and then slid away from his, leaving him feeling hollow, cutting him to the bone. She stalked into the lounge.

Hell, he hadn't meant to be callous.

But no one walked away from him. He headed after her, stopped when he saw her sitting on the couch leaning forward with her head in her hands.

His formidable chief of operations? His sexy responsive lover? Which? The lines had suddenly blurred and he didn't know which was more important to him. All he knew was, he wanted her in Sydney to find out.

She looked up and saw him watching her. "You have no heart," she said, and Lewis knew that if he didn't give her something, something of himself, he'd lose her.

He sat down beside her, and she watched him, that same dark disappointment in her eyes. Her hands twisted in her lap. "What made you so hard?" she whispered.

"I've had to be."

Jacques de Vries was Lewis's whole reason for living for the past two years. Now that he'd vanquished that septic thorn in his side, the sensible thing to do was to set some more goals, purge the revenge he'd supped on for two years.

Or else, with too much time on his hands, he was in danger of falling for a beautiful blonde with summer-blue eyes.

Lewis had never told another soul about his checkered childhood. He shied away from why he felt compelled to tell Madeline now. He wanted to take his time with her, and for that, she'd need to be in Sydney, so he'd better start making up for hurting her just now.

She arched one dark brow, waiting for him to speak, to lay bare his past.

"Jacques de Vries killed my father."

She exhaled slowly, her lips parting.

"Not what you expected?" he asked lightly. "I discovered that charming piece of news a couple of years ago, while identifying the body of my brother, whose death Jacques also had a hand in."

Madeline drew her legs up under her and leaned back in her seat, her eyes on his all the while.

Start at the beginning, he thought. "My father and Jacques were business partners in the early eighties. They ran a transport company taking aid throughout the African continent. We, my parents and I, lived just outside Nairobi."

It was a great life for a boy. Kenya was so colorful, the people warm. Lewis and his parents weren't rich by any stretch, but comfortable enough to have a great old house on the outskirts of town, with a housekeeper and cook. Lewis attended a school in Nairobi and spent every other minute having adventures.

"But one day, when I was seven, the police came for my father and threw him in jail, charged him with stealing the aid supplies and selling them on the black market. Jacques was in France, visiting his wife. My mother tried to get some help, some answers, but no one helped. After a week or so, she took me out of school and back to Australia."

Lewis had fought long and hard to be able to stay, wanting to be close to his beloved father. He never even got to say goodbye.

"She dumped me at my grandparents' house in Sydney, and that was the last I saw of her for months. She went back to see what she could do to get him out."

It was the worst time of his life. His grandparents were dour people who'd never approved of his father. They thought taking his young wife and child to Africa was irresponsible in the extreme. They enrolled Lewis in school and refused to let him speak of his father. He hated their deathly quiet house with the big ticking grandfather clock and all the surfaces gleaming, stinking of polish.

"When my mother finally came home, she was pregnant and deeply depressed. She hadn't been able to get my father released and had to trust that Jacques would pull off some miracle. She tried to prepare me for the worst. At the rate justice moved in Africa, it could be years before we saw him again."

All their money was tied up in the company. As much as both he and his mother hated staying with her disapproving parents, they were destitute. He'd never stopped nagging her to leave, felt bad about that now, but he hated living there so much. His mother knew, as he did not, the practicalities of being on her own with one child and another on the way.

"When Ed—my brother—was a couple of years old, Mum went on a benefit and we moved into a small flat. I think the grandparents were glad to be rid of us by then."

His mother never emerged from the depression and as soon as they moved away from her parents, she began drinking. Many days, Lewis bunked school to keep an eye on the toddler because his mother was trawling the town for money for drink, or passed out in bed. But he had to be careful. The grandparents were suspicious and he knew they would bring in the authorities if there was any question she wasn't looking after the boys properly.

"My father died of cholera, but we didn't find out

for a long time. He was still in jail with charges pending, but no conviction. It was like everyone just forgot about him. Poor Ed never even knew his dad.

"The next few years were hard, moneywise. Mum stuck Ed in child care and did a bit of cleaning. I had a paper round, but a lot of the money went on drink. And Ed was growing up wild." He smiled fondly. "He was trouble from the day he was born, always wanted what he couldn't have. When he started school, he'd just take things from the other kids if he wanted them. I had permanently bruised knuckles from keeping the school bullies away."

Madeline's leg moved out casually and her sock-covered foot nudged his thigh. He looked down and rubbed his knuckles. "Everyone said he was weird looking. He had this round head…" Lewis was too ashamed to tell her the truth. The bullies said Ed stank. He stank because he wet the bed every night of his life, and at thirteen or fourteen, Lewis didn't have the common sense to insist he shower before going to school.

"Ed inherited Mum's depression, I reckon," he said slowly, not keen to go into too many details. He recalled one day finding his brother drunk on the dregs of a bottle of whiskey his mother hadn't finished the day before. The little boy was only seven or eight years old.

When Lewis did go to school, he never knew what he would find when he got home. Sometimes there was a man, as drunk as his mother. Often he found her facedown in her own vomit. He and Ed would drag her down the hallway into her room, then Lewis would clean her up, put a pillow under her head and blankets over her and leave her to sleep it off on the floor. Once he got bigger, of course, he was able to wrestle her into bed himself.

He looked up to find her watching him closely. "I looked after them, I suppose. No one else was going to.

"I left school at sixteen and got a job as a storeman for a courier company, but with me out of the house all day, Ed hardly went to school and Mum didn't bother working anymore. But things picked up. With some help from my boss, I started my own business at eighteen, a courier franchise. We just kept speculating, and pretty soon the money was pouring in. I'd made my first million by the time I turned twenty-three."

No matter how good things were, his mother was still a drunk—just a better-dressed drunk with a better address. "But Ed," he said sadly, "he got away on me. He abused drugs for all of his teens."

The nights he cruised Kings Cross in the city looking for his younger brother would have numbered in the hundreds. There was no question of his leaving home—who would keep an eye on the other two? That put a dampener on his love life for all of his twenties. Since Lewis never knew what he'd find when he got home from work, there was no way he'd bring a girlfriend into the mix.

Then things looked up for a while. "Ed suddenly decided when he turned twenty he'd had enough of the drugs. He was a whiz with IT so I gave him all the encouragement I could.

"I finally got my own place at the ripe old age of thirty. Mum still drank but she went to AA meetings and she met a fellow drunk. They're still together, still drinking, but they have each other and a nice house to get blotto in."

Madeline smiled bleakly. Lewis bet she was thinking how different her straitlaced childhood was compared to his. How could two families be so very different and yet both dysfunctional in the extreme?

"And then a couple of years ago, I got a call from the cops, or Interpol or something, saying I had to go to Singapore to identify Ed's body. It was a drug overdose. I couldn't believe it. He'd been clean for three years."

He felt her foot pressing his thigh again and absently dropped his hand onto it and left it there. He wouldn't bother telling her about the horror of it all. Being classified as guilty by association and enduring strip searches in both Singapore and when he came back to Australia. He wouldn't tell her how much of a failure he felt as he stood over his little brother's white, lifeless body in a morgue far from home.

Her foot moved under his hand, pressed against his leg. "Why?" she whispered.

He shrugged. "I couldn't make sense of it at the

time. It took weeks getting through the formalities, bringing the body home, dealing with the cops there and in Australia."

"Your poor mother," Madeline said quietly. "Poor you."

Grief and guilt had consumed him, but he'd had to be strong for his mother, who went absolutely blotto. At one point, he seriously considered having her committed or put in rehab or something.

"A woman—Natasha—turned up at the funeral, said she was a friend of Ed's. I...got to know her."

Lewis wasn't proud of himself for the way he'd behaved. Natasha was French, beautiful, wild. After the stress of the last few weeks, he surrendered to a crazy lust. She was exotic and intense and they spent a week in bed before he started to wonder if she really was crazy, or worse, on drugs like Ed.

"She wanted to meet my mother, so one day I took her there, and suddenly she was screaming at Mum, she attacked her, slapped her, I had to haul her off. Ed wasn't my father's kid at all. He was Jacques's. She was Ed's half sister."

"After I'd thrown Natasha out, my mother confessed all. Jacques was kind, the only person in Nairobi who tried to help her make the authorities understand that her husband wasn't a crook. But nothing happened. Day after day, she visited the prison, pleaded with every authority she could think of. Jacques told her bribery was the only way, so she did that, too. The lawyers didn't want to touch the case. Nothing happened, everyone just kept saying come back tomorrow, maybe something will happen tomorrow."

Madeline shook her head with a sad smile. "That's exactly how some countries work, and not just in Africa." She shifted to lean her back against him with her feet up on the other end of the couch.

"Finally my mother snapped, I suppose." And Jacques de Vries was there to pick up the pieces, he thought bitterly. "Jacques 'comforted' her. But the moment she told him she was pregnant, he threw her out. He didn't want an affair with his jailed business partner's wife. He went back to his wife and child in France. Mum had nowhere to go but home. He gave her a few thousand, nothing like her share of the business, and she gave up, came home and tried to cope best she could."

"No wonder she was depressed," Madeline murmured. "What happened to Natasha?"

"She was heading back to Singapore when I caught up with her. She said she had proof that it was Jacques, not my father, who'd been responsible for ripping off millions of dollars worth of aid. She couldn't prove it, but suspected he'd bribed police and insurance officials. But she did have documents showing he'd received a vast insurance payout for the company when it folded. He went back to France, divorced his wife and set up his hotel corporation with the proceeds of the transport company, plus, I suppose what he got from his Black Market dealing. Silly bugger left a lot of the paperwork in the family home, which is how Natasha got hold of it."

"Can you prove it? Clear your father's name?"

The million-dollar question and, for a long time, his greatest desire. His poor father rotting in jail for years while his best friend and partner lived it up. No family to support him... Lewis inhaled deeply. If there was any way he could achieve that now, he'd be a happy man.

"It's—complicated. I hired some investigators. Their findings and some of the documents Natasha came up with would have made a pretty good case against Jacques, if I wanted to bankroll it, which I did. But some of the documents had my mother's signature on them. She swears she knows nothing of the fraud, but she had signed things, with Jacques's supervision. She thought they were gift certificates he told her would help pave the way for Dad's release. She certainly didn't profit from the insurance payout or after the company was wound up. Jacques told her he'd lost everything, too. I'd like nothing better than to see him behind bars." He gave a short, sharp laugh. "Actually I'd like nothing better than to see his eyes bulging with the pressure of my hands around his neck."

It had taken superhuman control the day of the Executive Committee meeting not to do that very thing when he went to see the man before publicly ousting him.

"But I can't be absolutely sure that the authorities wouldn't go after my mother."

Madeline snuggled in closer and he heard her yawn. "So you went after his company instead."

His arms tightened around her. "*My* company," he growled. "Born of the destruction of my family."

They sat quietly for a few minutes and Lewis wondered if she'd dropped off to sleep. The fire was toasty and he felt tired himself. He hadn't been counting, but he reckoned he was on the debit side of hours of sleep since he'd arrived in Queenstown and met Madeline Holland.

She suddenly heaved a great sigh while he rested his chin on her hair. "But I still don't understand why Ed did what he did."

Her hair smelled like apricots. "Who knows? Natasha contacted him by e-mail and said she knew who his real father was, and to meet her in Singapore. She told him Jacques's name. That's all I know for sure. I think he confronted Jacques and things went badly, leaving Ed so distraught he took some bad drugs. That's my personal view, but there could be any number of things. Jacques denies meeting him in person though admits Ed contacted him by phone. Whatever the chain of events, something led to Ed taking a massive dose of heroin, a dose he must have known, with his experience, would kill him."

"Well, what did Jacques say when you told him you knew about him?"

A fist of hate squeezed his heart but he was too tired to pander to it. "Laughed in my face and said good luck proving it."

"What about blackmail—" a yawn caught her unawares "—can't he be persuaded with the proof you have?"

"Really, Ms. Holland." Lewis chuckled. "The way your mind works." He'd spent months weighing up his options before settling on taking the man's company. "Jacques believed he was untouchable, but he's quite capable of taking everyone, my mother included, down with him. My way took a long time, but that's all right. I won."

A log shifted in the grate, sending a shower of sparks up the chimney. Lewis's hands were clasped around her middle, and now Madeline covered them with her own, stroking slowly.

"Am I forgiven," he murmured into her fragrant hair, "for being heartless before about your mother?"

Her hands stilled. He heard her long breath in and the rasp of his chin on her hair as she nodded.

"You're forgiven," she said simply.

Nine

Madeline woke to find herself spooned by a warm body, an arm lying heavily around her waist. It took a second to understand where she was—the couch in the farm's living room. As to why, the facts took their time seeping into her languorous brain.

She remembered most of the life story he'd told. Weird how his mother's guilt and shame shaped her children's lives, with striking similarity to her own. She understood better now Lewis's need for revenge, his ruthlessness when something distracted him from his goal, his scathing lack of sympathy for weakness.

Such a responsibility for one so young: hiding his home life from the world; eking out a living to save his family from Social Services, the poor house; death's embrace due to drink and drugs.

His hand moved, shredding her thoughts. The fingers spread slowly and it was impossible not to flinch in response to a heartbeat suddenly gone from a walk in the park to a canter, in one second flat.

They'd snuggled down together in the chill of a dying fire and he'd finished his story. She couldn't think of anything useful to say so had just leaned into him, giving him her warmth, hopefully her comfort. They must have fallen asleep. The last thing she recalled was the perplexed tone of his voice saying that he'd never told a soul what he'd told her tonight.

Lewis gave a beefy sigh behind her, arching so that the length of his body settled warmly against her back. His spread fingers curled into her diaphragm, cool even over her clothes. At some stage, he must have grabbed the blanket he'd used the night before on the end of the couch and spread it over them. But Madeline wasn't feeling the cold at the moment. She sucked her gut in, not to get away, but to contain the feeling of him holding her there, just below breasts that were suddenly wide awake.

It was a strange feeling waking up with a man beside her—well, technically behind her. Not something she'd done more than three times in her life.

She didn't want to move.

Lewis's lower body stretched and hunched into the dip under her buttocks, sending an eruption of unaccustomed early-morning desire welling up. Her nipples hardened, pushing against her bra and sweater.

Don't even think about it! They'd had their final night. How much perfection could a man and a woman want? It was batting against average to try for three perfect nights in a row.

"Good morning," Lewis mumbled into her ear.

Madeline squeezed her eyes shut and pulled a face to stop herself from groaning. Her ear turned out to be another erotic zone of hers, she'd discovered when she discovered Lewis. She tried, she really did, not to respond, to pretend she was asleep. Anything not to give in to something she already knew would be sensational.

He hummed deep in his throat, a sound of pleasure, contentment. That's all it was, she told herself. You can't sound contented if you're excited. Unless you were going "Mmmm" rather than humming. Like her, he was only half awake, warm, comfortable. Not aroused.

Except there was no point denying that she could feel his arousal. Especially since she couldn't resist pressing her behind up against it.

Just checking.

Lewis continued his gentle wake-up assault on her senses, and she pretended she was dreaming, a hot, sweaty dream that necessitated his plundering under her clothes and palming her breasts while she tried her best to grind him into the back of the couch with her backside.

It was like a dream come true when he finally began stroking her intimately, and then when she felt him hot and heavy between thighs that were mysteriously bereft of clothes, gliding back and forth, leaving her shuddering in jerky uncoordinated ecstasy so quickly, it made her head spin.

The only thing that could improve on the dream was when he was inside her, pressing her down; miraculously finding him inside her, snug, on an angle she hadn't felt before, liking it, moving with it, loving it—until they fell off the couch and hit the floor with a whump. And she couldn't pretend anymore that his weight on top of her hadn't caused a stampede of breath from her lungs, and then that she was laughing out loud, great gasps of it as she dug his elbow out of her stomach and fought with the trousers shackling her legs.

Couldn't pretend that she didn't see the fun in his eyes change to awareness and then, shockingly, to tenderness that made her heart bleed as he linked their fingers and slid over her, inside her again. Stilled, all fun gone in a slow lingering kiss, and then began to move, slow, deep, deeper.

She wished she was dreaming because she didn't want to see what she saw in his eyes. She saw all the things she felt; tenderness, liking, respect, safety. Wanting to support him, needing his…

Needing just a bit faster to stroke that pleasure point there, there and again there. Oh! Don't think, just feel, don't stop, and she spun out as he lifted her and crushed her to him, wrapping her up tightly, and came himself with a gusty sigh of pleasure and relief.

She lay there listening to his heartbeat, knowing she didn't want to look into his eyes again, she had to pull back, keep something in reserve or she would lose her heart.

She had lost her heart.

She knew it because of the pain that arrowed there when he disengaged himself, when his body left hers and she knew, without a doubt, that this was the last time, even though the other night had been the last time. Just as exquisite as all the other times, but with the added dimension of real caring, real feeling. Real heartache.

Lewis leaned back, smiling a little. Madeline ducked her head. She had to because her eyes were filling and there was no way in the world she would cry in front of him. But he was quick to call her on it. He moved his head sharply to put it in her line of vision. "Don't do that. Don't ever regret this."

She shook her head, looking down. "It's too late for regrets," she mumbled, knowing he wouldn't have a clue what she was talking about. How could he know that with their lovemaking today, she had fallen in love for the first time in her life.

She was too vulnerable, too needy to be with him now. She would not become one of his projects, his fixer-uppers. Maybe one day, she'd get off this emotional roller coaster that had kidnapped her lately and be the strong, competent, pragmatic woman she knew she was. But for now she was a puddle of emotions, and Lewis needed strength.

Then his phone was ringing and he was rising in a swathe of blankets and mismatched clothes, leaving her exposed and feeling silly. She let him have the bathroom first because the New Zealand-based directors had just hit town and wanted to re-schedule the conference call earlier and meet with him beforehand.

At least, she thought as she sat waiting for the coffee to drip, he'd have the comfort of familiarity. Soon he'd go home to his apartment, his city, his office. He'd call up whatever woman he was squiring around for a date. He'd visit his mother.

Whereas Madeline was starting from scratch. Floundering. She'd left a great job, was about to turn down an even greater job, been made a laughing-stock, discovered her mother was not only fallible, but scarily mortal. And now she had the memory of making love to Lewis on this couch, in front of this fire. And the thing that terrified her the most was the possibility that she wouldn't even be left with those cherished memories if she couldn't extricate herself from the contract of sale.

Lewis came into the kitchen looking gorgeous and clean, and swallowed half a cup of coffee. "Lewis, about this conference call…" Madeline began. There was no point in him going through with this thing with her when she would never be part of the team.

"Not now," he said quickly, banging his cup down. "I'm going to that conference call and I'll come back with the desired result, and then we'll talk, all right?"

As if she had much choice, with him already halfway out the door.

But then he stopped, came back, lifted her out of the chair with one arm around her waist, kissed her soundly on the lips and plopped her back down again.

"We'll talk," he repeated, his eyes serious. "Keep your phone on."

Maybe, Madeline thought, still breathless from that kiss. They'd talk of her mother, and why Madeline was having second thoughts about the opportunity of a lifetime to reach the very top echelon of the corporate world in Australasia. They'd talk about how good the sex was and how she'd never be happy as a small-town girl. But they wouldn't talk of the real issue.

She had to stay; he had to go. His businesses, his life, were there. And Lewis had spent his life looking after the needy, and, ashamed as she was to admit it, she was needy right now. Her life was out of control and she couldn't be the strong, competent woman he needed and wanted.

And that hurt like hell because the only other thing she knew for sure in this helter-skelter life of hers was that she was in love with him.

Her phone rang. It was the reporter for the local paper. He wanted to "give Madeline a chance to put her side of the story" and to comment on Lewis's statement about their relationship.

She was so not ready for this.

It was the moment of truth.

A sudden realization of what might happen if she refuted his statement, told the truth, trickled through her thought processes. Lewis would be angry. He would hate that she'd slapped his attempt to help down and that she'd rebuked him in public. He'd be pissed that he'd gone to bat for her with the directors for nothing. He wouldn't want her for his COO anymore. He wouldn't want her.

She haltingly agreed to meet the reporter later that day at an Internet café in town.

"Sorry, Ms. Holland." The real estate agent put his phone down with an apologetic look. "The lawyer says it's all confirmed. There's nothing you can do."

Madeline stared at him blankly. "But…I only signed the papers yesterday." Or was it the day before? So much had happened in the last day or two, she couldn't be sure. "How can it have gone through so quickly?"

"The sale and purchase agreement you signed accepted the purchaser's offer and their conditions. It's a binding contract. As I said before, the only one who can break the deal at this stage is the purchaser, and only then if he can't meet the conditions you accepted on the contract." He picked up some papers and straightened them, avoiding her eyes.

Madeline knew when she was being politely dismissed.

"Can't I talk to someone? To the manager of the development company?"

He looked down at the contract in front of him. "The signatory is an agent designated by the development company, PacAsia Enterprises. He probably isn't even part of the company. You can look PacAsia up in the company register, if you like." He stood up. Clearly the conversation was at an end. "But I warn you, big pieces of prime real estate don't come up here very often. Frankly, a development company would be crazy to let that go."

Madeline got the same story at the lawyer's. "What if I offer the purchaser a sweetener to crash the contract?"

The lawyer pursed his lips. "That's your prerogative. But if they don't accept, then there is nothing you can do."

Madeline was being naive. She also realized that the real estate agent or the lawyer were hardly likely to assist her to do away with their fees.

With a heavy heart, she wandered the streets until she found herself outside the Internet café where she was supposed to meet the reporter. She was an hour early, but got herself a coffee, logged into a computer and then keyed in the name of the development company.

Frustrated beyond measure, she drummed her fingers as the register took its sweet time loading. Now, when she had finally made the decision to stay in Queenstown, it seemed everything was conspiring against her. Where would she live? She knew it would break her heart to leave her family home.

PacAsia Enterprises Ltd. finally came up on the screen.

Madeline wrote down the registered address. No phone number, three directors, she scrolled down to the share parcels and saw that one company held all the shares. She read the name, checked, and read it again.

PacAsia Enterprises shares were all owned by one company, Pacific Star Enterprises.

Madeline read it again, very slowly, just to make sure, then, with icy expectation, she raised her eyes to the directors listed.

"Goode, Lewis Jay."

The hum of chatter around her faded as her heart sank somewhere close to her ankles.

Lewis Goode had stolen her farm.

The two New-Zealand-based directors sat at the boardroom table with Lewis. The conference call had been rescheduled a number of times, but finally they were underway. Lewis prepared to receive a grilling.

The directors were concerned about the conflict-of-interest angle—how much did Madeline Holland know about Lewis's corporate takeover bid at the time she applied for the job? His explanation was pretty much what he'd outlined to Madeline last night.

Most of the directors seemed amenable. The New Zealand directors had flown down as a show of support because they knew of the opposition he would face from at least two of Jacques's old cronies. These two directors spoke up now, offering the view that Madeline was not COO material for allowing herself to get into this position.

"Oh, for Christ's sake," Lewis growled. "There were two of us in the elevator. How come my morals haven't come into question?"

Suddenly the door flew open with a bang, and Madeline stalked in.

"You bastard!" she said in a breathy exhalation, her eyes blazing.

Quick as a flash, Lewis hit the mute switch.

"You won't get away with it."

Lewis stood with a quick glance at the two men around the table. "Please, excuse me." Then he was on his feet, striding purposefully toward her, his lips flatlining. Every muscle vibrated with anger. He grasped her above the elbow, turning her smoothly, and whisked her outside.

Hardly pausing as he pulled the door closed behind, his relentless momentum took them to the wall opposite and then, when she had nowhere to go and no room to move, slapped his hands on the wall at both sides of her head.

Her eyes spit sparks of blue, and she opened her mouth but Lewis intended giving her not a second's grace. He could not recall when he'd last been so angry. Probably not since the night he discovered Jacques de Vries's part in his father's and brother's deaths.

"I will *not* be interrupted, do you hear?" He delivered the forceful missive in a deadly low voice that surprised even him.

Madeline's eyes were wide, but he could see she was determined and not the least intimidated.

"You. Bought. My. Farm." The words left her mouth equally forcefully like four quick smart slaps to his ears.

Shit!

"You do not interrupt me," he gritted, "in an important meeting like this when my balls are being nailed to the floor because I am standing up for your integrity."

Madeline blinked. For one fraction of a second, he saw the slightest hesitation, then it was gone. Doubt smoothed away, replaced by cold and composed anger. "Don't do me any favors, *Mr.* Goode. I want my property back, and you are going to assure me of that right now."

She was good. In spite of the tension, Lewis was once again awash with admiration. Madeline

Holland was his chief of operations and he was damned pleased about it.

Not that he was going to let her know that right now. "I will discuss this *private* matter with you at a more opportune time, Madeline." He stretched the syllables of her name out, reminding her that he was the boss and she the subordinate.

She opened her mouth to protest but he was quicker. "Go home and I will see you there later." He pushed away from the wall and stood glowering at her, waiting for her to make her move. He would call security before he allowed her to burst in on him again.

Madeline drew herself up to her full impressive height. He'd never wanted to kiss her quite as much as he did at this moment, but he carefully concealed it.

"You won't get away with this, Lewis," she said, her chin rising. "You are going to cancel that contract and you are going to do it today."

Lewis looked down his nose at her. "We'll see. Don't you ever interrupt me like that again."

They glared at each other for a moment more, battle lines drawn, then she nodded briskly, turned on her heel and strode off down the hall, the tight A-line skirt hinting at a femininity that even her brisk, angry, businesslike stride couldn't hide.

And Lewis watched her all the way, not because he was afraid she would return once his back was turned and burst in on them again. He watched her because his blood was pumping, most of it in a south-ward direction. If it was not imperative that he get back to his very important conference call, he would have gone after her and taken her up against the wall.

The interlude did more to help his case than anything he'd come up with before. He came back into the room fired with admiration and so adamant that Madeline Holland would turn out to be the best COO Premier ever had the privilege to employ. The directors were convinced. And the meeting concluded soon afterward.

Now he just had to convince Madeline herself.

He'd bought the farm on the day the story about him and Madeline in the elevator broke. He intended nothing to get in the way of her coming to Sydney, certainly not a bit of scandal. And hey, the place was on the market, it was fair game. Over the last day he'd congratulated himself on his decision, especially when she began to vacillate about staying here with her mother. Taking the farm off her hands, and for a very fair price, was just one more reason for her to pack up and go.

Perhaps he should have told her, especially before making love to her this morning. That wasn't a meeting of strangers, nor a planned last fantasy romp before they knuckled down and got on with the job. This morning had a whole Pandora's box of feelings about it. Something had changed. It went deeper than wanting her or professional admiration.

This morning he'd felt warmed by her. He'd gone to sleep with her on his mind and woken the same way. And he wasn't afraid to have it happen that way again. And again.

Naturally, once he'd started loving her, he could hardly spoil the moment by telling her he'd bought her farm out from under her.

He called her as soon as the two men left the room. Now that his task had been finalized to a satisfactory conclusion, it was time to start eating humble pie. Madeline was going to Sydney with a clean slate, a bit of office gossip aside, which he knew she'd deal with easily. So what need did she have for the farm? Her mother certainly wouldn't be using it.

He dialed her number, but she was either on the line or the thing was turned off. Lewis decided against leaving a voice mail and chose to go and have a celebratory lunch in the hotel restaurant. Just as he finished, someone approached.

"Are you trying to catch us out?" Kay smiled brightly and pulled out the chair opposite.

Lewis pushed his empty plate aside and smiled at her. "The Akaroa salmon was excellent. Will you join me for dessert?"

"I've eaten." Kay signaled the waitress. "I will have a coffee if you don't mind."

They chatted for a few minutes and then Lewis asked if Kay had seen Madeline. "I've been calling for an hour, but no luck."

Kay looked away, her eyes on the approaching waitress. After they'd given their order, Kay cleared her throat. "She came to see me after she'd…surprised you in the boardroom," she finished judiciously.

Lewis nodded, smiling pleasantly. "I trust she won't make a habit of surprising me in boardrooms. Any idea where she is now?"

"Well, she had an appointment with a reporter, but that was an hour or so ago."

He gave her a sharp look. "What the hell is she talking to a reporter for?"

"In case you hadn't noticed," Kay murmured, "you two are all the rage at the moment. He contacted her. I believe his reasoning was that the media have had a say, you have had a say, it was time Madeline put her side of the story across."

Lewis folded his arms and studied Kay thoughtfully, careful to conceal the little bit of unease that skittered through him. He knew Madeline wasn't happy about lying.

What if she told the truth, that there was no relationship and the security tape and reports of passionate liaisons in plush resorts were the real deal. Lust, pure and simple.

That would certainly put a fly in his ointment.

"Don't worry," Kay said soothingly. "Madeline's the soul of discretion, even if she may not be that happy with you at the moment."

And Lewis stopped worrying because this was Kay, Madeline's oldest and dearest friend. And she didn't look worried.

Ten

Three hours later, Lewis walked off the flight from Queenstown and stepped into Christchurch Airport, ninety minutes before his flight to Sydney.

This time there was no smile for the hostess in the Pacific Star lounge. He didn't bother with the buffet. He stood by the window, looking out at the tarmac, wondering how it had all gone so horribly wrong.

The reek of betrayal clung to his nostrils. He'd never felt the need to share his personal history until last night. Some misguided notion that he wanted Madeline to understand him, and wanted to distract her from the emotion and distress of the last couple of days.

Lewis had only just started thinking about relationships when he'd moved into his own place, finally believing that his brother and mother were safe. A scant year wining and dining and fighting off the gold diggers, and then Ed up and died. From then on, he lived and breathed revenge.

He wasn't looking when he arrived in Queenstown, and then he found her, wanted her, and now—well, fool that he was—he might just be in love with her.

Darkness gathered on the tarmac, as grey as the doubt flirting with his mind. What if he was wrong, what if it wasn't her? Surely he hadn't confused tough and capable with cruel and calculating?

Of course it was her. He'd bought her farm. She'd told him, in front of his colleagues that he wouldn't get away with it. And then she went off to have a cozy tête-à-tête with the reporter.

It was unbelievable how quickly everything had unfolded. The reporter and the Sydney police broke all records, but wasn't that the way when a public persona was involved? He'd assumed, when he saw his mother's number come up on his phone, she was calling about the scandalous reports in the media.

In fact, she'd called to tell him she'd been arrested on historical insurance-fraud charges, and all because of her son's pillow talk. He really had to stop sleeping with women. They weren't good for his mother's health. She'd endured a verbal and physical assault by Natasha and now Madeline's actions had her sitting in a police cell.

How quickly Madeline had wound her way into his heart. It was a short, sharp reminder that looking out for number one was the only way to go.

His boarding call came and Lewis took his phone out to turn it off just as it rang.

"Where are you?" Madeline asked, her voice cool.

"Christchurch Airport." He waited, tapping his passport and boarding card on his leg.

"Christchurch? I don't understand."

Again he grappled with doubt. Was it just wishful thinking to wonder if Natasha could be the culprit? But as much as she hated her father for abandoning her mother, she'd begged Lewis to be discreet about his revenge. Could Jacques himself have had an attack of conscience?

Lewis rejected that out of hand. Madeline was the only possibility.

"Lewis? I thought you were coming out tonight. Only, I have to go out now, the Women in Business thing."

"Did you enjoy your little talk with the reporter?" he asked acidly.

Another pause, longer this time. He pictured her lovely heart-shaped face, shadowed with guilt.

"Nothing left to say?"

"Lewis…" Her voice was barely audible. "I'm sorry. I did what I had to do. The truth always comes out in the end."

Lewis laughed harshly. "In this case, the fantasy was better than the truth."

He heard her indrawn breath and it tore at him, but now that she'd confirmed her betrayal, he would excise her from his life as if she'd never existed. "I have a scoop for you, Ms. Holland. You're fired." He paused, waiting for a sign that she cared about that. "The Waterfront will be sold and the other two hotels torn down as soon as I can get a buyer for the land." A clear sound of distress came down the line but he ignored it. "And…" He paused one last time, just for the hell of it. "You have one month to get off my farm!"

Madeline slid down to the floor in a daze, still holding the phone. His words could not have slashed her deeper.

In the space of a couple of minutes, righteous anger had turned into confusion and then fear, heartbreak, letdown. Her guilt about publicly refuting Lewis's statement faded. His reaction was way over the top, undeserved.

Madeline had lost everything. Her job. The respect of her peers, who would now hate her for losing their jobs. Her home. And her love.

Her throat constricted and tears prickled at the backs of her eyelids, but she wouldn't cry, couldn't. In half an hour, she'd be standing in front of a gathering of up-and-coming businesswomen, telling them how to have it all.

When she'd lost it all.

Things in Madeline Holland's world could not get any worse—or could they?

Two days later she heard the door knocker and watched Kay wend her way through the throng of people in her living room at the farmhouse. Another plate of scones to go onto the already laden table. Well-wishers from all over town and country bustled around talking quietly, while she stood like a dummy, fortified by their kindness and affection.

Her mother had lost the fight against a sudden and savage bout of pneumonia. Lucky, as it turned out, when the chest X-rays showed a pair of lungs covered in tumors. Big, inoperable tumors.

Who were all these people? She'd had more hugs and kind words today than she'd accumulated in twenty-eight years. So much for thinking she didn't have a home. Home was here—not the farm, sadly—but this town, these people whom she, and her parents before her, had grown up with. They stood in the hall, fussed around the table, sat on the couch that she and Lewis had— But she wouldn't think of that now.

"No, sadly," she said to old Mrs. Lucan, who lived down the road. "I won't be able to stay here, but I will be staying in Queenstown."

"The farm is too big for you on your own." The old lady nodded understandingly.

"I sold it when I thought I was leaving, then I tried to stop the sale, but it's too late now."

Someone touched her arm, and she turned to find Brian Cornelius, her mother's friend.

Her mother had told her that her lover's name was Brian. The nurse said he visited Adele every Sunday. Suddenly it all fell into place.

Madeline wanted to thank him for visiting her mother regularly, for sticking with her and trying to show her she was not a bad person, even though she was sure Adele would have saved her choicest missives for the man who'd toppled the Bible Lady from grace.

She put her arms around him and kissed his cheek. "Perhaps one Sunday, you could come out and we could scatter Mum's ashes together."

Brian squeezed her hands, unable to speak for long moments. A gentle smile creased his face. "I'd like that," he said. "Very much."

She squeezed his hands back. "I think she would, too."

Kay pushed through the crowd, holding out the phone. "It's Lewis," she whispered close to Madeline's ear. "Want me to tell him to get lost?"

Madeline closed her eyes for a long second. There had been little time to dwell on the heartache. She had heard via Kay that apparently Lewis's mother had been arrested on suspicion of insurance fraud. She'd felt for him and wished his poor mother strength to survive. But thoughts of his mother only brought back thoughts of hers.

She took the phone. "Hello, Lewis."

"Madeline?"

At least he didn't sound hateful and cold like he had last time she'd heard his voice.

"Sounds like you have a houseful."

Was he ringing to gloat or to offer commiserations?

"Madeline, I'm—sorry. Truly sorry."

That didn't sound like gloating. Thankfully, Kay must have told him. Madeline hadn't quite worked out how to say it, how best to get her tongue around it. My mother has died, has passed away, is no longer with us…

"Thank you, Lewis. How is your mother?"

Lewis cleared his throat. "It's been tough, but she'll be all right, as long as the Scotch holds out."

Madeline smiled. "Look after her. You never know…" Her voice hitched and she took a couple of steps away from her neighbor, battling for control.

"Madeline, those things I said, I'm just…I don't know how to make it up to you."

She didn't know, either. And she didn't want to even think about it right now. Her system was overloaded.

"Bye bye, dear," one of the well-wishers said, pecking her on the cheek.

"Thank you for coming," Madeline said, hugging her back. "I'll see you Wednesday."

"Yes," Lewis said. "I'll be there Wednesday. I can't leave until I've got Mum's lawyers sorted out."

"*You're* coming on Wednesday?" Madeline asked, bemused. "For the funeral?" It was nice to get the sympathy call, but she hadn't expected that.

There was a long silence. "Lewis?" she asked, thinking she'd lost the connection.

"Funeral? Your mother's funeral?" he asked quietly.

"Yes," she said, noting another carload of well-wishers coming up the driveway. "I have to go, Lewis. Thank you for calling."

"To the Holland funeral," Lewis clipped out, sliding into the back of the airport cab.

"You're late," the taxi driver commented, pulling smartly away from the curb.

Late. Too damned late to recognize that he loved Madeline Holland.

Lewis had no idea what her reaction to his presence at her mother's funeral would be. He hadn't spoken to her since the day her mother died. For all he knew she would order him from the church.

Trying to clear the mess Jacques de Vries had left in his sudden and unexpected attack of conscience had taken forever. He couldn't leave his mother to battle the legal stuff while she was in such a state. The insurance company had not opposed bail as long as she handed in her passport. It wasn't over, but finally he could leave her with her boyfriend to drink away the horrors of the past week.

The church overflowed out into a pretty little courtyard, so he stood in the drizzle like a hundred other mourners and listened to the last of the service through a tinny intercom system.

Then the church organ started and the crowd in front of him sidled back to let those inside out. Lewis stood firm, his head well above most of the crowd, copping his share of curious looks.

They would be even more curious if Madeline ignored him or gave him his marching orders. No more than he deserved for his appalling behavior.

Then she was there, walking slowly toward him, looking as if a puff of wind would blow her over, except Kay had a tight hold of one arm. Her long black overcoat almost dwarfed her and contrasted sharply with the pale skin of her face. The freezing drizzle drifted down onto her shining, golden bare head.

She looked so sad. Lewis hoped she'd had time to make her peace with her mother before she died.

Then her face raised and she looked full at him and held his gaze. Her step faltered for a second, and he wondered if she'd turn from him, or be vague and polite like the other day on the phone. If he knew her at all, she would hold strong, and certainly wouldn't countenance any public display of emotion.

But she didn't stop, and she didn't stop looking at

him. In fact, as the crowd parted before her, she kept on coming and walked straight into his arms.

Lewis wrapped her up and held her tight, resting his chin on her head. She stood quietly, her face hidden in his shoulder, and slid her arms around his waist. He never wanted to let go.

He accompanied her to the graveside, along with the whole town, it seemed, even in the freezing grey drizzle. He stood by her side at the community hall, where ladies bustled around making hundreds of cups of tea and setting out plate after plate of food. And when most people had left and Kay asked if Madeline wanted to stay with her tonight, she shook her head. "I want to go home."

The rain had stopped and a watery sun broke through the clouds as the cab turned into the long driveway of the farm.

"Going to be a nice sunset," the driver commented before they alighted.

Lewis set about lighting the fire in the lounge and the coal range in the kitchen. He had no idea what he was doing here, if she wanted him to stay, if she wanted to talk.

Madeline came out of her bedroom. She'd changed into jeans, a black high-necked jersey and a white cardigan over it. They stared at each other for a moment.

Holding his gaze, she smiled at him tremulously. "Thank you, Lewis."

He raised his brow. For what? Accusing her of doing something she wasn't capable of? For not listening and going behind her back? Or for not telling her how he felt about her after making love with her on the couch? Who would have thought a crummy couch and a patch of floor could totally overshadow the much grander fantasies of the past?

"If you don't mind," Madeline said, her eyes drifting out to the veranda, "I'd like to sit outside for a while, watch the sun go down."

He stepped toward his coat, but she held up her hand. "Alone, if that's all right. I have a goodbye to make."

He nodded, but picked up his coat anyway and slipped it over her shoulders, wanting to be close to her in some small way. "I'll bring you out a drink."

"Thanks. A glass of wine would be lovely."

He took the wine out to her, then went back inside, poured himself a glass and pulled a kitchen chair up to the old coal range. But his eyes kept wandering out to where she sat, with her back to him, on a rocking chair on the veranda. The chair moved slowly. She faced the turbulent sky as the sun slid slowly down behind the Remarkables mountain range.

She was saying goodbye as the sun went down on her mother's life. Although he badly wanted to be with her, comfort her, he knew she needed some time and space to say her goodbyes in private.

* * *

Madeline pulled Lewis's coat up around her neck and ears, inhaling him, rocking slowly on the creaky old chair. The ache of unshed tears was almost painful.

"You did us proud, Mum," she said, knowing her mother would have been delighted at the unprecedented turnout. Adele Holland loved a crowd. "Just think how many sinners you could have lambasted today." She ticked off a few names on her hands, only feeling a little silly.

The lowering sun arced through the clouds and sent a ray of yellow from the step to her feet. "Goodbye, Mum," Madeline whispered, feeling the tears back up, her throat swelling. "I love you and I'm sorry, and thank you for telling me you were sorry. Perhaps now we can be friends."

She kept her eyes on the last streak of orange in the sky, focused on it until her eyes nearly crossed and there was nothing but dusky grey black.

Gone. All gone…she wrapped her arms around herself and finally gave in to the tears.

The door opened and then Lewis was in front of her crouching down, his hands on her knees. "Just let me hold you."

Without waiting for her reply, he slid his hands under her, lifted her up, then turned and sat with her in his arms.

The unaccustomed slide of tears down her face, the unfamiliar feeling of being wrapped up in security and strength, only made her cry more. Maybe she was entitled. She snuggled into his warm chest and cried all the tears she'd never been able to cry. All the times she'd missed home, missed her parents, wondered why she was so terrible that her mother didn't seem to love her at all. She'd thought she had time to mend bridges but she'd run out of time. She cried for the longest time, and Lewis held on tight and rocked her slowly and said nothing, which was just as she wanted it.

A long time later they went back inside and he refilled their glasses while Madeline mopped at her face with tissues.

"Sorry about that," she said as he settled down beside her.

"What, for being human?"

A niggly little headache squeezed behind her eyes. "I'm sure that's the last thing you needed after the few days you've had."

He'd borne her tears well, she thought, but that was the very reason they couldn't be together. Lewis needed strength and reliability and Madeline was fresh out.

She tossed the tissue on the fire. "How's your mother?"

"The police are satisfied there was no intent to defraud. It's up to the insurance company if they want to take it further."

"But how is *she*?"

Lewis gave her a crooked smile. "Relieved. Old."

She smiled into the fire.

"Who would have thought," Lewis commented, "that old Jacques would get an attack of conscience at this stage of his life?"

"Jacques?"

"He turned himself in," Lewis told her. "I don't suppose you've had much time to read the papers."

She shook her head. "So he turned himself in for bribing the officials to keep your dad in prison?"

"That, the insurance fraud, bankrupting the company, selling on the black market." Lewis frowned. "Why do you think I blamed you for Mum's arrest? I never, in my wildest dreams imagined he would come clean to the authorities. I thought you'd told that reporter everything."

Madeline turned to face him. "You thought I dobbed your mother in?"

He spread his hands wide. "You were the only one who knew the whole story, except Natasha, and I couldn't see her telling after all these years." He shook his head. "And you hated me, remember, for buying the farm?"

Madeline gave a resigned laugh. "And here I was thinking you were angry because I'd told the reporter the truth about our relationship." With her mother's death and then the funeral arrangements and constant visitors, she wasn't even positive that her comments had made the papers.

It all seemed rather silly now, anyway.

Madeline took a deep breath. "Lewis, I want you to sell the farm back to me."

"I bought it because I wanted you in Sydney."

She'd worked that out for herself when she calmed down.

"Is that what you really want?" Lewis asked, tucking a strand of hair behind her ears.

"Yes." She nodded emphatically.

He gazed at her for a long time and she didn't look away, even though she knew she must look disgusting. Puffy eyes and blotchy skin, if the rumors were true about crying.

There was no disgust in his eyes, only serious contemplation.

She'd appreciated his support today. She appreciated all the support he'd offered in their short acquaintance. As he'd told her once, he'd had plenty of practice.

"Confirmation is tomorrow," he told her. "I won't confirm. The contract will be cancelled."

"Thank you." Her voice was thick with relief. Now she knew she could bear anything.

"Is there no hope?" he asked. "Of you coming to Sydney? The things I said were just heat of the moment. You're not fired. I won't be closing the hotels."

Madeline stared into the flames and finally felt a lick of that old familiar confidence and assurance that she'd worked so hard to attain. "But I don't want to be an executive anymore," she said brightly, delighted that she had found it. "I know, it must seem like a waste, but I'm tired of being rootless. Of living in hotels. Tired of making decisions, big important decisions that affect hundreds of people, when I don't make any decisions in my own life, my personal life."

She squeezed his hand because he looked bereft and she wanted to show him that she was happy. "I want to stay here, start something. Maybe a homestay or a boutique hotel…I don't know exactly. A weekend retreat of some kind, become a life coach maybe—don't laugh!" How utterly ridiculous after the mess she'd made of her own life.

"I'm smiling," Lewis said, "because it sounds perfect for you. Remember our first night at the retreat? You told me then you wanted to teach, but not children."

Her eyes shone. "Did I?" She hadn't remembered many details except the physical ones! "I want to get to know people, maybe have a garden, gossip amongst the neighbors. Live amongst these people who loved my mother, no matter what." She sighed. "You know, I might put some money toward rebuilding that old church."

Madeline was so excited with her new plans, so relieved that she had her farm, her home back, it took her a while to notice how pensive Lewis looked. Her brow furrowed. There were plenty of corporate executives out there. He'd have no problem finding someone to run his hotels.

"Do I have any place in this?" he asked finally, and reached out to take her hand.

She lifted his hand in hers and linked their fingers. "Life's been so crazy lately. I only know two things. One is that, for now, this is home. I don't know if it will be forever, but for now, I need to be here." She kissed his fingertips and then gave him a sidelong look. "Of course, you could visit. I happen to know this great place in the mountains."

He dragged her hand over to his and repeated her actions, kissing her fingertips, one by one. A sultry slide in her stomach told her that he was thinking about four-poster beds and candlelight and probably garter belts.

"That would get the town's tongues wagging," he smiled. Then he sobered. "What's the second thing you know?"

Oh, damn. Why had that slipped out? How could she tell him she loved him with all her heart when they couldn't possibly be together? Not seriously, not in any other than as long-distance lovers, who would eventually tire of the distance and find someone to build a future with.

She and Lewis dealt in fantasy and they were good at it. There was no harm in giving in to fantasy once in a while, although she wrote a mental memo to use a bit of discretion next time. But Madeline wanted reality now, even if it hurt.

"Ahh." She held his gaze, biting her lip. Diving into the unknown. "Just that I love you." Something shifted in his eyes, like someone had pressed the alert button. "Don't worry," she said quickly. "It doesn't obligate you to anything."

Lewis sighed heavily and she took that as an admonishment.

"Must you always try to beat me at everything?" he asked, squeezing her fingers. "The ski field, the luge…"

She grinned, glad the awkward moment had passed. "I never beat you at anything."

His smile faded slowly. "You would have made a great COO."

"Thanks." She would have, but that wasn't who she was anymore.

He shook her hand gently to get her attention. "Would you marry me?"

Her head jerked up and she was shocked to see that his face was perfectly serious. "What?"

His eyes bored into hers. "Well, you beat me to what I was about to say—that I'm in love with you— so I thought I'd get in first with the proposal."

"Before I…beat you…" she stammered, her heart suddenly rapping on her rib cage. "You love me?"

"Absolutely," Lewis said with typical directness. "When I saw you at that retreat, I thought you were the most beautiful thing I'd ever clapped eyes on. It truly felt like we'd stumbled upon a real-life fantasy, you, the surroundings, the way we met—and the sex was out of this world. It was the whole deal." He smiled. "Like a dream, it could not have been improved upon."

Madeline smiled, nodding. That was pretty much her take on that night.

"But one night of bliss was never going to be enough. I watched you work, I saw you in pain, we comforted each other. I fell in love, but events tore us apart and I'm so sorry I left without getting the facts, giving you a chance. I don't want to spend another minute apart."

Madeline's eyes filled quickly with tears again. This crying jag was getting out of control. She never cried. "I'm not one of your projects, am I? Something to fix up because I'm having—was having—a hard time lately?"

He shook his head slowly and she recognized the same look in his eyes as the other morning, when she'd finally admitted to herself that she loved him. They'd crossed the finishing line together, it seemed. "I've just felt so low with everything that's happened, and I couldn't bear it if you saw me as a burden. I'm normally a very strong capable person— and I will be again…"

"Madeline, you have all the qualifications for the job." He kissed her fingers again. "Say yes, and we'll stay here and fix your place, *this* place up, into anything you want."

Her heart had already overflowed at his declaration of love and his proposal. But to think he wanted to stay here on the farm with her… The tears spilled over and she brought their hands up to her cheek, held them there. This really was the best fantasy she could ever have dreamed up.

"How can we stay here? Your businesses?"

"Modern communications being what they are, I can run most things from here. We'll work it out." He brushed the tears from her cheeks. "I own an airline so the commute won't be a problem."

"You've made me the happiest person in the world," she murmured, cupping his cheek and leaning in for a tear-glazed kiss. Then she pulled him to his feet and they walked to the window and looked out at a near-full moon glistening on the lake, throwing the jagged edges of the mountains beyond into blurred, sullen shadows.

"That's a billion-dollar view," Lewis said, pulling her close.

"It's more than that," Madeline said softly. "It's where fantasy meets reality."

* * * * *

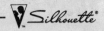

SPECIAL EDITION

A late-night walk on the beach resulted
in Trevor Marlowe's heroic rescue of a
drowning woman. He took the amnesia
victim in and dubbed her Venus, for the
goddess who'd emerged from the sea.
It looked as if she might be his goddess of
love, too…until her former fiancé showed
up on Trevor's doorstep.

Don't miss

THE BRIDE WITH NO NAME

by *USA TODAY* bestselling author
MARIE FERRARELLA

*Available August
wherever you buy books.*

REQUEST YOUR FREE BOOKS!

2 FREE NOVELS PLUS 2 FREE GIFTS!

Silhouette® Desire®

Passionate, Powerful, Provocative!

YES! Please send me 2 FREE Silhouette Desire® novels and my 2 FREE gifts (gifts are worth about $10). After receiving them, if I don't wish to receive any more books, I can return the shipping statement marked "cancel". If I don't cancel, I will receive 6 brand-new novels every month and be billed just $4.05 per book in the U.S. or $4.74 per book in Canada, plus 25¢ shipping and handling per book and applicable taxes, if any*. That's a savings of almost 15% off the cover price! I understand that accepting the 2 free books and gifts places me under no obligation to buy anything. I can always return a shipment and cancel at any time. Even if I never buy another book, the two free books and gifts are mine to keep forever.

225 SDN ERVX 326 SDN ERVM

Name	(PLEASE PRINT)	
Address		Apt. #
City	State/Prov.	Zip/Postal Code

Signature (if under 18, a parent or guardian must sign)

Mail to the **Silhouette Reader Service:**
IN U.S.A.: P.O. Box 1867, Buffalo, NY 14240-1867
IN CANADA: P.O. Box 609, Fort Erie, Ontario L2A 5X3

Not valid to current subscribers of Silhouette Desire books.

Want to try two free books from another line?
Call 1-800-873-8635 or visit www.morefreebooks.com.

* Terms and prices subject to change without notice. N.Y. residents add applicable sales tax. Canadian residents will be charged applicable provincial taxes and GST. Offer not valid in Quebec. This offer is limited to one order per household. All orders subject to approval. Credit or debit balances in a customer's account(s) may be offset by any other outstanding balance owed by or to the customer. Please allow 4 to 6 weeks for delivery. Offer available while quantities last.

Your Privacy: Silhouette Books is committed to protecting your privacy. Our Privacy Policy is available online at www.eHarlequin.com or upon request from the Reader Service. From time to time we make our lists of customers available to reputable third parties who may have a product or service of interest to you. If you would prefer we not share your name and address, please check here. ☐

SDES08R

KATHERINE GARBERA

BABY BUSINESS

Cassidy Franzone wants Donovan Tolley,
one of South Carolina's most prestigious
and eligible bachelors. But when she
becomes pregnant with his heir, she is
furious that Donovan uses her and their
child to take over the family business.
Convincing his pregnant ex-fiancée to marry
him now will take all his negotiating
skills, but the greatest risk he faces is
falling for her for real.

**Available August
wherever books are sold.**

Always Powerful, Passionate and Provocative.

COMING NEXT MONTH

#1885 FRONT PAGE ENGAGEMENT—Laura Wright
Park Avenue Scandals
This media mogul needs to shed his playboy image, and who better to tame his wild ways than his sexy girl-next-door neighbor?

#1886 BILLIONAIRE'S MARRIAGE BARGAIN—
Leanne Banks
The Billionaires Club
Marry his investor's daughter and he'd have unlimited business backing. Then he discovered that his convenient fiancée was passion personified…and all bets were off.

#1887 WED TO THE TEXAN—Sara Orwig
Platinum Grooms
They were only to be married for one year, but this Texas billionaire wasn't through with his pretend wife just yet.

#1888 BABY BUSINESS—Katherine Garbera
Billionaires and Babies
Convincing his pregnant ex-fiancée to marry him will take all his negotiating skills. Falling for her for real…that will be his greatest risk.

#1889 FIVE-STAR COWBOY—Charlene Sands
Suite Secrets
He wants her in his boardroom and his bedroom, and when this millionaire cowboy realizes she's the answer to his business needs…seduction unfolds.

#1890 CLAIMING HIS RUNAWAY BRIDE—
Yvonne Lindsay
An accident leaves her without any memories of the past. Then a handsome man appears at her door claiming she's his wife.…

SDCNM0708